WEEDS THROUGH THE FLOORBOARDS

A Novel

JONNA TRUSTY-PATTERSON

ISBN 978-1-63784-365-9 (paperback)
ISBN 978-1-63784-597-4 (hardcover)
ISBN 978-1-63784-366-6 (digital)

Copyright © 2024 by Jonna Trusty-Patterson

All rights reserved. No part of this publication may be reproduced, distributed, or transmitted in any form or by any means, including photocopying, recording, or other electronic or mechanical methods without the prior written permission of the publisher. For permission requests, solicit the publisher via the address below.

Hawes & Jenkins Publishing
16427 N Scottsdale Road Suite 410
Scottsdale, AZ 85254
www.hawesjenkins.com

Printed in the United States of America

"Memories not remembered are often
the safest memories of all."
—Jonna Patterson

FOREWORD

There are pivotal moments in time that I have chosen to store away in my mental library—out of sight of others who I fear might reach for them, thumb through the rough pages, judge them, and recklessly fold the corners down into perfect, geometric triangles as if to mark their place in my life.

These are moments that perch quietly on a dusty, unkept shelf that is vividly cluttered by other memories, waiting for their own turn to be read. I can imagine these memories challenging one another in efforts to be read first, because they are ignored and, quite frankly, they feel lonely. They have been there the longest, like unwanted orphans with nowhere to go, waiting for closure.

The memories are methodically and tightly lined, one right next to the other, allowing no room for others to be added. Each memory is sealed with a beautiful cover, very similar, I would assume, to the one enveloping this book. And embedded on the spine of every memory, an inscription, penned in the finest gold thread, an honest token of remembrance lest I forget.

But as each memory is pulled from the shelf, the one next to it loses its balance and must lean on the others for support. And eventually, all memories tumble and dissolve into total disarray and chaos. And as each memory is read by an innocent passerby, it nervously awaits a gracious literary review as if on the coveted red carpet of the much-anticipated springtime Mental Illness Awards on NBC.

> "An atrocious and staggering attempt at
> persistent antidepressants, antipsychotics,
> mood stabilizers, and stimulants!"
> —Nadine, Idaho

> "Could not put it down! A must read for anyone
> needing to feel better about their own fuckery."
> —Linda, Pennsylvania

> "Cheap and scathingly oppressive and self-
> pitying. It is almost too good to be believed."
> —Carolyn, New York

PART 1

Chapter 1

A THORN IN MY SIDE

I am in fourth grade.

I am sitting in Ms. Thornson's class at Oakland Heights Elementary. It is Tuesday. This memory grants to my mind an incisive day of Tuesday. Tuesdays are careless. Tuesdays should be Thursdays or any other day but Tuesday.

The hard camel-colored desks with frigid metal backs are arranged in the unfortunate shape of the letter *O*, allowing students to absently stare at one another as if to send a warning signal to Ms. Thornson's next victim.

The hollow crevice of my desk overflows with broken pencil scraps, one-inch crayons, a tattered baby-blue milk card with hole punches, and a delicate red-and-green paper chain meant to adorn a Christmas tree. I had so carefully cut the even strips of construction paper and stapled the pieces, taking precious time to interlock each piece with the next—red, green, red, green, red. The shortened strand now protrudes from my desk, broken, crumpled, and falling apart, just like how everything in life eventually falls apart.

Ms. Thornson paces the inside of the circle with her tribunal wooden pointer, which she theatrically slaps into the palm of her hand in militaristic four-second rhythms. On the bottom half of her awkwardly shaped body, she attempts to wear a knee-length black pencil skirt three sizes too small made of a Sears polyester and I-need-an-orgasm blend of cheap fabric. On the top half, she dons a crisp white cotton long-sleeved blouse to cover her inability to be anything but hidden from her rage and anger. Ms. Thornson is as bitter as the pungent odor of raw berries that have failed in life and have never reached their full potential.

Someone has neatly and painstakingly carved the letter *H* on the very right tip of my worn wooden desk. I am eloquently tracing the letter back and forth with my right index finger. This movement appears to calm me on certain days, especially on Tuesdays.

I consider this indentation to perhaps be a message to the entire world or simply a message to the fourth-grade class of tiny, innocent souls who have yet to be completely fucked up by the unpleasantries and impending evils of life. Poor darlings. They simply need patience. Their time will come. My time just happens to arrive earlier than most.

My imagination runs wild with the intricate carving, and I envision someone signaling to me a secret code of grand significance.

Hi?

Hello?

Hate?

Hell?

Help?

I am surrounded by the intense smell of Elmer's rubber cement in an old glass jar, tragically worn erasers that carry the scent of a poorly lit match, and thin, color-edged pencil shavings that remind me of the dead mulch in my grandmother's never blooming Jesus Saves Garden. The cursive alphabet on display calmly embraces the room and connects into one unending line that fits perfectly around the classroom from *Aa* to *Zz*.

I am jealous because I don't fit perfectly anywhere.

WEEDS THROUGH THE FLOORBOARDS

While my right fingers are tracing the mystery character, I am twisting my hair with my left index finger, a coping mechanism that has worn a permanent scar on the left side of my middle finger. I often brush over the signature callous, rough bump with my other fingers so I know I am still alive. Although this well-rehearsed circular, twisting motion calms me, it also reminds me of my insides—twisted and breaking.

"Ruby Jane Clancy, stop twisting your hair! Such a stupid child! Stupid, I tell you!" Ms. Thornson screams at me with spit spewing in all directions.

She slams the pointer harshly onto my desk, inches away from my tracing fingers. All eyes land on me. In my mind of magical escapes, I boldly leap out of my seat. I place my small hands around her throat and press firmly until she cannot breathe.

When someone cannot breathe, they cannot tell.

My magical escape continues with bravery as I respond.

"I am so relieved you asked. No one has asked, and I cannot tell. Did you not see the clue I carved into my desk? Help? Everything is wrong! Why don't you know?" I retaliate as I press harder around her sagging neck with the oversized pearl choker.

I would like to incorporate, "You stupid, cunt-fucking bitch." However, I am most certain this unfortunate phrase has yet to exist in my repertoire of nine-year-old words.

Instantly, the pressure from the do-not-tell secrets is exploding from my chest and climbs its way into the world through a swarm of unstoppable tears followed by immediate regrets. Alice Sansbury sends me a malicious grin and covers her toothless giggle with the cuff of her ugly, dirty beige winter coat. I hate Alice Sansbury.

I release the twists from my finger and lean into my desk to locate my Scholastic book order form, where I have exactly $4.29 to purchase my *Nancy Drew Mystery Stories*. I am humiliated, defeated, embarrassed, and unwanted. Once again, Nancy Drew saves the fucking day.

I fucking hate Alice Sansbury and Tuesdays.

Chapter 2

GRANDDADDY TUESDAYS

After school, I walk to Ms. Wanda's house, where I will stay until Momma picks me up after her day shift at the local bank. I don't mind the walk. I appreciate the delay. I pretend I am on an extravagant adventure as I leap over broken pieces of sidewalk, balancing on the edge of the curb as if walking on the jagged edges of Mount Rushmore, a historical landmark that I recently discovered in our *Encyclopædia Britannica* collection.

Eventually, I am stepping through a small, unkept yard that will bring me to the front steps of Ms. Wanda's home. The house is ancient and unkept. It feels like a secret. It is trimmed with chipped dull-gray paint combined with a lazy effort of boring white shutters, most of which are hanging in a most dramatic fashion. Even they don't want to be there.

I don't knock. No one ever knocks. The front door to Ms. Wanda's house is always open. I assume she leaves all exits open in the event we need to escape. This reminds me of a flight attendant standing at the front of an aircraft, modeling the aircraft exits. She is elegantly polished and beautiful and wears a perfectly pleated dark-blue dress with shiny silver wings attached to the lapel.

"There are four emergency exits. There is one at the front of the cabin, two over the wings, and one at the back of the cabin. Please take time to review the exits, as the closest one may be right in front of you."

When I enter the home, there is a palpable clutter of years of neglect. There is an olive-green love seat with three wires protruding on the left side. A beveled red candy dish holds old, orange-wrapped butterscotch candies that have become softened by age. There is no TV, no radio, and no joy, only a wall of dreadful wood paneling that longs for newness.

"Well, hello there, Ruby Jane. I was beginning to wonder where on the blessed earth you were. You shouldn't lollygag, young lady. You make everyone fret something fierce. Would you like a snack?" Ms. Wanda asks in a sweet, motherly tone.

I, however, am not fooled. I know why the front door is left ceremoniously unlocked, and so does she.

"No, thank you," I reply as I fish through my *Scooby-Do, Where Are You!* schoolbag for my library book.

Ms. Wanda glances directly down to see me carefully open my book, Nancy Drew's *The Secret of the Forgotten City*. I appreciate the author's carefully selected words for this title. I am forgotten. I have secrets.

Ms. Wanda shoots a glare my way as I settle down on the shag navy-blue carpet to read.

"You should think long and hard, child, about what you read. Why, Ruby Jane, that is simply the devil's work. The devil will get his grip on you. You keep filling that brain of yours with nothing but false prophecy and lies? It's nothing short of a disgrace. The Bible is the only way to heaven, and entertaining that silly mind of yours with trash will land you a guaranteed place in the eternal damnation of the flames of hell. Your momma not teach you nothing, child?"

While Ms. Wanda's decision is to ridicule and suffocate me with her uninvited preaching, my decision is to remain silent. I am pretty sure I can simply ask the devil if this impromptu sermon can actually be validated and hold truth. The devil lives here, in this house, near the exit row.

"Did you hear what I said?" she continues to press, becoming angry at my silence.

Again, I remain silent and say nothing. Some memories are best left in silence.

"Child, you look at me when I am talking to you! You disrespectful, heathen brat! You are gonna burn in the lake of fire reading all that garbage. That's the devil's work, I tell you! Now go on in there and pray with Granddaddy. Pray that Jesus will not damn your sorry ass to the depths of fire and brimstone!" she demands while reaching up and softly touching a picture of white Jesus on the mantel.

She smiles as she traces his kind face and the prayer-clasped hands with her fingers and gently dusts around the Savior with an old, worn white cloth. Jesus looks like Andy Gibb.

She grabs my arm and physically pulls me toward the old, warped brown door with the faded gold knob and opens it for me to enter. I walk into the darkness of routine. She looks over her shoulder as I sit on the edge of the bed. Then she closes the door.

I am alone. I hear only the sounds of her singing resonating from the living room.

"There is power, power, wonder working power. There is power in the blood of the lamb."

He enters from the back of the room. He always enters from the back and gradually creeps through the darkness. I always know when he enters; it is more what I smell than what I feel. He is wearing stained gray tweed pants and a musty plaid sweater that smells of mothballs and body odor. His bulging black glasses no longer fit his face, and they barely balance on his nose. His breath is putrid and reminds me of black licorice.

His smile is toothless as he pushes me down onto the threadbare bedcover and unfastens his belt. The air leaves the room. I am searching for the exit row. I close my eyes.

I fucking hate Alice Sansbury and Tuesdays.

Chapter 3

DIRT TEA

It is revival week at the Pine Creek Pentecostal Church in Yell County. Being raised in Arkansas means you know that there are two things you simply don't miss in Yell County. The all-you-can-eat buffet at the local Shoney's on Wednesdays after church services and revival week at the Pine Creek Pentecostal Church.

Pine Creek Pentecostal Church stands proudly in the middle of a creamy, mint-green pasture, with a beautiful cross that rises to the heavens as if a beacon to lost souls in the night. The enormous cross is painted snow white, just like the soul we seek to achieve while here on earth.

The weathered-looking church pew cushions are burnt orange, a strategic decision to remind us sinners of the color of the actual flames of hell. The old wooden pews creak with any human movement as if you are a burden to be carried.

At the front of the sanctuary, carefully placed on display above the organ, hangs a wooden sign with miniature rivets that allows numbers to slip effortlessly through side by side. There are always two numbers to be displayed. The first number is the attendance for the church service. The second number is the offering.

Today, the display reads:

49
672.23

We all know that old lady Baker gave most of the money. Her husband, Denni Ray, killed himself in the garage last year. They found him hanging from the ceiling rafters with a strand of Christmas lights wrapped tightly around his neck. Rumor has it, he left the lights plugged in, as if he was blinking out a colorful fuck-you SOS. I mighta done the exact same thing if I had to live with old lady Baker.

I am sitting on the third row next to Beatrice Rhones. Beatrice is in my fourth-grade class. She has soft long brown hair that falls over her shoulders. She always smells like fresh lemons and Pledge furniture polish. I think Beatrice Rhones is the most beautiful girl I have ever seen.

We've come prepared. Not prepared in the Second Coming of Christ prepared kind of way. We have hidden small pieces of paper in our Bibles somewhere between Leviticus and Deuteronomy. We have learned to be careful, because our Sunday school teacher, Brother Bill, always says that an inattentive soldier in the army of God becomes an attentive student of the devil.

Beatrice takes my hand; our fingers brush together, and she tenderly slides the piece of paper into my palm, a familiar dance we will continue throughout the night, back and forth. I cautiously unfold the paper, cupping my palm over the written words.

> Beatrice: Do you think Jeff is cute? Circle yes or
> no.
> Me: No.
> Beatrice: Do you like red or yellow?
> Me: Red.
> Beatrice: I am bored.
> Me: I am bored.
> Beatrice: I hate this. B. O. R. E. D.

Our visiting evangelical leader, Pastor Bartlett, concludes his salvation recruitment efforts. He raises his arms to the sky as he cries for our deliverance. He then pats his dripping-wet face dry with a small, dingy white handkerchief he keeps in his suit lapel.

The altar call has begun. Floods of sinners fill the aisles as they march like Onward Christian Soldiers to the front of the church to confess their transgressions and plead to God and to members of the congregation for forgiveness.

Mr. Crayswell, our PE teacher, stumbles to the altar.

"I had a moment of weakness and ate Saturday supper at the Holiday Inn buffet, where they serve alcohol."

Insert dramatic, audible gasps from the audience.

"I am a sinner and ask for forgiveness."

Brother Bartlett looks to the audience and firmly says, "Brother Crayswell has confessed his full transgressions. All in favor, say aye."

The entire congregation responds with an affirmative.

"Any nays?"

Brother Bartlett submits to the audience, because our salvation depends on everyone but us.

Carl Brooker, who works at the local Grab and Go, confesses that he danced at the Knights of Columbus Veterans' Benefit and played three games of bingo and begs for forgiveness for the sins of evil and gambling.

Darla Rae Taylor admits that she succumbed to wickedness and went to the local Picwood Theater and saw the movie *Grease*, which had dancing and heavy petting. I am envious. I am not allowed in the movie theater.

I want to confess to Granddaddy Tuesdays. But Mondays, Wednesdays, and Thursdays are now available on the weekly schedule; and I am almost certain there would be no affirmative ayes from the members.

I feel an overwhelming urge to slide into the aisle and follow the masses to the front, where I, too, will apologetically proclaim to the entire congregation, "I want to marry Beatrice Rhones because I love her, and I want her to be my wife!"

Deep down, I think Andy Gibb Jesus would understand.

*****

I spend most weekends at my grandparents' house, a one-bedroom shack two miles off Route 101, hidden somewhere in the middle of unexceptional and Six Flags over Jesus. There is no street sign. There is no mailbox. There is no physical address. None of this is needed. No one is allowed inside the Kingdom without a personal invitation.

There is, however, an impressive trailer that is nestled quietly in the backyard. It is light brown, like the tip of the Winstons my daddy smokes, and the roof is covered with a shiny metal that reminds me of the outside of a Ding Dong wrapper.

I often dream of running away in this trailer. I imagine what an adventure it would be to have a house on wheels, where I can just wake up and move wherever I want. I can run away from my secrets or even toward them if need be.

While I keep lots of secrets, it is no secret that Grandma is simply and utterly batshit crazy. We all know Grandma is housed in the trailer when she has one of her sinking spells, as Momma calls them. It's kind of like a Holiday Inn Express getaway, but without the holiday part.

Lately, Grandma has been having more and more Holiday Inn Express moments, so Grandpa has taken the wheels off the trailer.

During her last Holiday Inn Express sinking spell, she damn near burned down the toolshed next to the Jesus Saves Garden because she thought a nice, raging fire would reckon my cousin Jimmy to fear hell due to his going to a Methodist church camp and all.

Grandma often sits on the tree trunk Grandpa has carved into a throne-like seat and preaches to her congregation, which includes only a few dead plants and whatever strawberries are left from the season before.

Momma drops me at the front gate and drives away. There is no need for conversation between Momma and Grandma. It only causes problems. I jump out of the car and run to Grandma with my arms wide open, hoping to be wanted.

"Grandma!" I shout in true excitement as I wrap my small arms around her knees.

She stands as stiff as a board in her faded lime-green bedtime robe that feels like a thick oversized mattress. Grandma wears this robe and this robe only. When I think about it, I have never once seen Grandma in any other apparel. I wonder if the robe is Grandma's very own signature hair twist bump that makes her feel calm and comforted, just like mine.

"Ruby Jane Clancy, what on earth are you wearing!" she says.

I can't tell if this is a question or an upcoming sermon.

"What? What do you mean?" I reply. "I am just wearing my playclothes."

"Why, I can clearly see your knees, Ruby Jane. What is the meaning of this? Did your momma deliberately send you like this to hurt me? Did she? Answer me. Is she mocking me? I swear, that woman has been a heathen in heat since the day she cut her own hair to spite me!"

I don't know how to respond to this unexpected venom clearly directed toward my own mother. Should I agree? Should I defend myself? Should I ask Andy Gibb Jesus? WWAGJD?

"Oh, never mind, child. Come on with me."

She reaches down for my hand and slowly leads me down the overgrown path that eventually leads to the shack.

"It is time for healing and repentance, and I need to prepare for our service."

I know what this means. We all know what this means.

Grandma crouches down on her hands and knees in the front yard and methodically pulls up long green blades of grass, flowers, and weeds, examining each one for miracle potential. She carelessly throws them in an old black iron pot to boil with water.

As the water boils, she stares into space, speaking with a sense of urgency in an unknown tongue that frightens me. At times, she becomes louder as she cries out and raises her hands, and her eyes roll into the back of her head. Then her words fade into the room, and then silence.

When the water finally rolls to a boil, she carefully pours two cups and delicately sets them on the table.

"One for you, and one for me," she offers in the kindest, softest voice.

She then leans into me until our noses almost touch.

"The Holy Spirit gives me the gift of visions, child, and the power to cast out demons and evil. Drink this tea, and don't you ever forget that we came from dust, and to dust we will return. We come from the earth, and from the earth comes all healing and salvation. God is the ONLY physician, Ruby Jane."

She blows softly over the top of the rusted tin mug. I follow her lead, blowing the steam that is rising from my cup. We sip in the hot liquid as it streams down our throats and into our lives.

"Oh, my sweet Ruby Jane, can you feel it? Doesn't this taste of power? Of faith healing? Of atonement and redemption?"

She closes her eyes and becomes entranced in something far bigger than me.

"You better get your life right with God now, Ruby Jane, 'cause the Rapture is coming, I tell ya. It is here, and I am chosen. I know these things, Ruby. God speaks to me. Can you hear him? Shhh."

She places her index finger over her mouth as if an invitation for me to listen. I hear only the grumbling of my empty stomach and the sound of an obnoxious bird in the distance.

"Did you hear that? He says he is coming, and he is taking us home. What glorious news. We are finally going home. Isn't that wonderful? Praise God. Praise his holy name!"

I feel like we should call people and let them all know so they can get right too.

Grandma smiles vibrantly as a small tear sets a joyful pathway down her cheek. Her face shows nothing but contentment and the purest of peace, and I want to believe this is all true. She is so beautiful when she smiles.

"Now drink," she says, encouraging me to finish my weed tea. "Isn't it wonderful?" she asks with no intended room for me to answer.

I nod with enthusiasm so she will be proud of me. But if truth be told, it tastes like dirt. It always tastes like dirt.

After our routine reservation at the Dirt Tea Room, Grandma and I head to the back porch. The porch is my favorite place to be. It makes me feel guarded and protected from the outside world. The porch has a screen that surrounds and encompasses the entire space. The heavy gray metal wiring is ripped throughout with several deep slashes that form the letter *X*.

It's no secret the screen metal was placed there to keep Grandma inside, and the slashes are there on account of her last spell. Grandpa forgot to remove his hunting knife, and Grandma decided she needed out. So *X* marks the spot.

She opens the freezer and pulls out the Neapolitan ice cream, which is cradled in a cardboard box that perfectly and colorfully matches the insides. Chocolate, vanilla, and strawberry. Brown, white, and pink. She hands me a spoon and gently motions for me to sit on her lap. We share the spoon, taking turns eating the ice cream right out of the cardboard box.

We only eat the vanilla. We are not allowed to eat the other colors. Grandma says it's on account of the dark being the color representing the souls of damned sinners and the pink being the color representing desire of the flesh.

You gotta be real careful when eating right out of the box. If your spoon accidentally touches the sinful colors, it's all bets off. But today is a good day. I don't touch the sin.

As the day comes to an end, it has become rainy and cold. The only heat is from the black wood-burning stove in the kitchen. I quietly make my bedtime pallet on the floor next to Grandma's bed. Grandpa doesn't sleep with her. That would be sinful.

"Grandma? If the Rapture comes tonight, will I go with you?" I innocently ask while closing my eyes.

"Well, heavens, no, not facing that way, child," she firmly responds. "You surely won't. Turn your head the other way. We must all be facin' east if we want to get in the Rapture."

I slowly and methodically twist my small body to the opposite side of the pallet. As I lay my head on the hard floor next to her bed,

I notice a small bundle of weeds pushing up through the floorboards. It's as if they hope to be part of the Rapture too. I take my small hand and ever so gently bend and mold them slightly so they are all facing east...just in case.

Grandma died two weeks later. I am confused and cannot help but wonder and anxiously question why I am not included in her Rapture. Wasn't she the Chosen One? Why would she not take me with her? Why would she just leave me here?

Grandpa found her in the Jesus Saves Garden with her Bible clutched to her chest. I did not have the nerve to inquire as to which way she was facing.

Chapter 4

HOPELESSLY
DEVOTED TO YOU

It is the summer before the seventh grade, and I've finally made a new friend. This is not an effortless feat when others are not a member of the Kingdom. We spurn any and all people outside of the Kingdom.

Her name is Amy Green, and she lives a mile from the old rock quarry, where I spend most of my days riding my bike, wading in the shallow pool of cool lake water, and Pentecostal-praying that Momma doesn't find me showing my legs around boys.

Swimming can be considered a sin depending on whom you ask but mostly depending on what you wear and who you are with.

Pentecostal Swimming Rules for Girls:

1. No bathing suits are allowed for any purpose.
2. No showing of any skin above the knees.
3. No coswimming. (Definition: Males and females may not be in the presence of one another during swimming activities of any kind.)

Pentecostal Swimming Rules for Boys:

1.   None

Amy and I ride our bikes to Mr. Jansen's corner market on Old Mill Road almost every day. Mr. Jansen has aisles of peculiar things that smell like fresh berries, cardboard, and sunshine. Behind the counter, he keeps the grown-up aisle—neatly stacked cartons of cigarettes, chewing tobaccos, cigarette papers, and matches.

It's no secret that Mr. Jansen also keeps a back room full of illegal liquor should one need a touch of this or a little bit of that. It's also no secret that Mrs. Jansen walks around the store sipping her touch of this or a little bit of that out of her Tanya Tucker–embossed cup that has bright-pink rhinestones around the lip.

We've just purchased two orange Fantas from Mr. Jansen when Amy asks, "Do you want to come back to my house? My parents are gone for the day, and I'm pretty sure my dad left beer in his refrigerator."

I automatically freeze.

"I'm not sure. I mean, I guess. I mean, I think that would be okay," I reply cautiously.

I am not certain if I am more shocked at the invitation to someone's house outside of the Kingdom or at the fact that someone drinks any sort of alcohol and keeps it in their refrigerator.

Amy hops on her bike and jets off so quickly I barely have time to confirm my beer-drinking decision or to catch up. The humid summer wind pushes into my face, and I realize I am completely unaware of the path I am taking.

In the Kingdom, the Path is far more complicated than an actual walkway. The Path is one of righteousness, which is to be committed to walk by God's side and to be loyal and faithful to him. The Kingdom Path reminds me of Grandma's Jesus Saves Garden, where planted among the strawberry vines there stands an old wooden signpost, the edges ragged with years of wear and tear. In Grandma's handwriting, embossed in heavenly-white paint, a sign reads, "Proverbs 3:6: 'In all your ways acknowledge him, and he will make your paths straight.'"

As I ride to my impending unrighteous field trip, I realize that for the very first time in my entire life, I am thrilled that for once, my path is crooked, unpredictable, and not fucking straight. We tire-skid into the driveway of an enormous home with a perfectly circular drive in the front. I like the feel of a circular driveway. It means you can change your mind.

I've never been in a house this large. I'm pretty sure this house is bigger than the entire Pine Creek Pentecostal Church. We walk around to the back, and Amy politely slides open the glass patio door, which allows us access into something so grand, I cannot find words.

It is a room full of brilliant lights, shining with delicate crystals and silver beads. They hang from the ceilings like the forbidden fruit on The Tree. In the middle of the room, there stands an ornate, felt-covered maroon pool table with feet shaped like a bird's claw. And off to the side? A real live jukebox.

I cannot breathe for a moment. I can only take in the grandeur of this exact moment in my life. I feel seen.

"Wanna hear some music?" Amy asks as she makes her way over to the fridge.

I don't know how to respond. I've not been allowed to listen to music—or the Sonnets of Satan, as Grandma coined it many years ago. Besides church music and hymns, I've only listened to what I could hear sneaking around and paying attention in shopping malls and grocery stores.

"Sure," I reply, acting as if I know every word to every song on earth.

I want to feel normal. I don't like being different.

Amy casually flips through the music selections, and suddenly, the jukebox lights up with the most beautiful notes and words I've ever heard. Amy opens the refrigerator and graciously invites me to grab a beer. I reach in and pick up a tall, thin, ice-cold silver can.

Amy takes the beer from my hand, pulls back the clover-shaped tab, raises it to her lips, and swallows, leaving a cute white foam surrounding her tiny mouth.

"Your turn," she says almost seductively, handing the beer back to me.

I take the beer, hold the inviting fragrance under my nose, and take a long, studious whiff. I've never smelled beer before. The aroma comforts me and smells of the local paper plant in the summer with a hint of fresh sawdust.

I raise it to my lips, tilt the can gently, and feel the coldness calmly run down my throat. My insides warm. My warm parts get warmer. I feel protected, like the beer needs me as much as I need it. I again lift the can to my lips and, this time, take the liquid in its entirety into my body.

Amy throws her hair back, and her long, slim body racks with fits of laughter.

"I fucking love you!" she manages to say in between snorting and trying to catch her breath.

"I love you too!" I politely reciprocate.

I lean in and softly place my lips on hers. She tastes like salt and summer. She reaches out and pushes me away so violently that my body lands into the jukebox.

"You fucking pervert! Get the fuck out of my house! You fucking fuck! What the fuck is wrong with you! Goddamn lesbian homo!" she screams at the top of her lungs.

She picks up another beer and hurls it at my head. I am rushing and scrambling, trying to find my entry point. My head is swimming from the beer, and my only need right now is to find the door...a door...any door...the exit row.

As I frantically search for my exit strategy, I depart while hearing the words musically ring in my ears, "Right now, there's nowhere to hide since you pushed my love aside. I'm out of my head. Hopelessly devoted to you."

I fucking hate John Travolta.

Chapter 5

PENIS LESSONS

It's officially been over a year since the Amy Green Homo Chronicles landed me into the prize, coveted role of Citizen Lesbian within this small-knit community. I don't mind. I kind of like feeling noticed. I am secretly hoping for a billboard on Route 101, one with my Glamour Shot picture that reads, "Does advertising work? It just did," like a recruitment agency for area lesbians in need of friends.

The beginning of high school brings all things new, like whispers and glances as I pass from class to class throughout the day. They rubberneck at times to gawk and catcall throughout the hallways of the school.

In my mind, I defend my honor and meet their catcalls with witty, savory humor that leaves them angered and annoyed. In my mind of magical escapes, I secretly imagine we are all guests on an episode of *Jerry Springer*, where I enjoy the overzealous attention but am at an incredibly high risk of royally fucking someone up at any given moment.

It's most peculiar. When you develop a questionable and raunchy reputation as a lesbian, sin tends to flock to you unsolicited. I am literally about to flock the flock out of the flock.

It is after school, and I am walking to the school bus, because I've aged out of the Granddaddy Tuesdays after-school program. Dewayne Mitchell makes a beeline directly toward me and marches straight up to my face. Dewayne is way older than me. He drives a shiny black Camaro with bright-red fire pinstripes on each side. Did I mention Dewayne Mitchell is the same color as his Camaro?

"Hi, Ruby. Whatcha up to?"

He patiently waits for me to answer. I, however, cannot.

"Wanna take a ride with me? See the sights…and smoke some weed? I got some Jamaican Red Hair that has your name on it—Ruby Red."

He softly reaches out his hand and brushes his fingers through my hair.

"I…I…uh, no. I need to get home. I, well, no. I am good," I reply nervously.

I sound like a stupid child lesbian basket case.

Dewayne doesn't budge. He gently touches the side of my arm, tracing my skin from the top of my elbow to the bottom of my fingertips, all while he looks straight into my eyes, winks, and uses his tongue to wet the lower part of his lips.

"I need to show you what you're missing. Ya feel me?"

My knees are visibly shaking underneath my Pentecostal pants.

"Midnight. Skyline Pass near the orchard. Don't be late, baby."

He walks away without allowing me to breathe a yes, a no, a hell no, or a maybe.

I am uncertain of what has just happened. I am frantic with what all this means and at the same time wondering what Dewayne Mitchell could ever want with me. Me? I am unwanted.

That evening, I lay completely motionless in bed with the covers pulled over my head like a tent we use at summer revivals. I am attempting to cover myself from things that are about to transpire. Am I going? Am I staying? What if I get caught? Do I care? Am I really missing something?

I glance at the clock located on my dresser. The bright silver numbers read eleven thirty, the only hint of light in my room. My heart is racing, and I can hear it beating in my eardrums. I look at the clock every thirty seconds, anxiously waiting for the numbers to change, or better yet, for my decisions to change.

I am waiting to hear the silence of our home. There is rarely silence when there are secrets. I slide out from the covers, fully clothed in a purple shirt I stole from the lost and found in the locker room at school. This well-thought-out, preplanned wardrobe makes my decision to sneak out premeditated.

The shirt has wide-open shoulders and a long, draping V-shape cut down the back, something one can never wear when you live in the Kingdom. I slowly and quite literally tiptoe down the hallway and through the kitchen to the front door.

I stop, remain still, and wait. One, two, three, four, five. I am counting the seconds it would take my parents to greet me if they, by any chance, hear me making really bad decisions in the middle of the night. When I am aware that no one has heard me, I slowly unlock the door and make my way into the unknown.

"And he shall direct your path." Whatever. Not in the dark, that is for sure. I cannot see shit. The walk to the orchard is pitch-black, and I try to make my way, staying hidden from any possible witness to my super bad decision excursion. I finally reach the orchard and plant myself behind a large, blooming shrub that leans against the gate at the entry.

Eventually, headlights shine from a distance and then slowly approach. Dewayne's car crawls right up next to me, and the passenger door opens.

"Hop in, baby," he gently entices.

We pull the car behind the rock quarry to an isolated area where all one can see is the bright moon and foreseeable uncertainty. Dewayne stops the car, kills the headlights, and cranks the music. He reaches into the glove compartment, an act that justifies his fingers sliding peacefully across my left knee. He casually pulls out a joint and places it between his lips without ever taking his eyes off me. I can smell the flint from the Zippo.

No words have been spoken. Words are overrated. He hands me the joint, and I take it. I confidently place it to my lips and inhale so deeply that my lungs burn from deep within, just like secrets.

Dewayne laughs and sweetly touches my hair. I like it...the joint and the touch. He opens his door, and his gaze lets me know he wants me to do the same. We seat ourselves on the ground behind the car. We can still hear the music from the radio.

Dewayne gently embraces my face with his hands. He places his lips on mine and sweetly kisses me, his tongue parting my lips and exploring my mouth, and I give in. As he moves closer to me, I feel the weed take over my entire body.

He kisses me tenderly and passionately, and his tongue travels from my mouth to any and all areas of my body that are unclothed. He then removes my lost-and-found shirt slowly and then my jeans. There is now a sense of urgency on both of our parts.

I lay anxiously waiting for what comes next. He continues to kiss me, gently holding my face with his hands. And as he finally places his hips to mine and presses his hardness into me, I groan. I feel a wetness between my legs that I've never known. He moves up and down, and I move with him, staying in cadence with his stride. It feels amazing. He feels amazing. Everything is amazing.

I don't recognize the noises coming from my throat. My heart races, and an intense rush slowly spreads throughout my entire body. All of a sudden, a sharp, sudden release of pleasure escapes as if it has been trapped, waiting for Dewayne Mitchell to answer and release.

"I fucking love you," he whispers in my ear.

All I can think about is Amy Green. Fucking bitch Amy said the same thing. No one loves anyone when they are just trying to fuck, and no one loves me. I am unlovable. I am lost between confusion and lust. I feel guilt. I feel good. I feel used. I feel wanted.

I physically release a huge sigh, and then I slowly turn my head to the side, in search of the exit row. My eyes eventually come to rest on a small bundle of weeds pushing up from the ground. I reach over and touch each one as if I am asking them to tell me their story. We all have a story. My story just happens to be made of secrets.

One of the weeds has a tiny yellow bud blooming from its tip, as if trying so hard to not give up. Even weeds need second chances, just like Tuesdays.

Chapter 6

LESBIAN TRAINING LESSONS

I spend every single Wednesday evening at church in PTC, or Pentecost Training Course. We all do. Just as athletes train for a coveted role in the Olympics, we train for our coveted role to enter the Kingdom. I am not very good at the Jesus Olympics, if truth be told.

I often contemplate what it is exactly that I am being trained to do. They will tell you that we are being trained to spread the Word of our Lord Jesus Christ to all sinners around the world. If you are not in our Kingdom, you will not be chosen for the Rapture.

I will tell you that I am trained seven days a week to be afraid, deathly afraid, of anything and anyone outside of the Kingdom. Whatever the motivation, they have been successful. Fear is an ideal motivation to not fuck up.

Tonight, Brother Eddie stands at the front of the sanctuary next to an old, faded white screen that, quite frankly, needs to be retired. He holds a remote control in one hand and a long wooden pointer in the other. He pushes the remote on the Kodak carousel slide projector, and the slides spin one after another—click, click, click—as he reminds us all of our duty and calling. This reminds me of an adult View-Master.

Annette Davis explicitly leans her mouth right next to my ear and whispers, "Do you think Brother Eddie still has sex with his wife? He looks like he would like little boys. Ya know? Of course, YOU would know. You probably slept with his wife, leeeezzzzzbooo."

She draws out this last word until there is no breath in her airway.

Without hesitation, I lean back to her, ease my mouth as close to her ear as I possibly can, and say, "You bet I did, and it was fucking epic. I came three times. Tag. You're next."

I place the tip of my tongue into Annette Davis's ear. She thrusts her head straight up and storms out of the church with a sense of urgency, wiping away the wetness I've created with the sleeve of her shirt.

After the Wednesday Slideshow Extravaganza, we all congregate in the Fishers of Men Fellowship Hall, where the Ladies of Zion Club serve bright-red Kool-Aid from a dingy plastic punch bowl they use for potluck suppers and last-minute weddings. There is a large platter of Hydrox brand Creme Betweens, which we all know are posing as Oreos. I grab a handful and slip out the back door.

I make myself comfortable behind the dilapidated shed that stores the church lawn mowers and yard equipment. I pull a well-secluded pack of Pall Mall 100s out from the loose wood, light one up, and take a long, deep, relieving drag.

As I fumble around with the pack, I catch a glimpse of the words "May cause cancer," which makes me want to inhale all the toxins even more. I love a good challenge.

It is at this exact moment that Annette Davis appears out of nowhere.

"Hey," she says softly, nowhere near resembling the dramatic exit strategy from earlier.

"What the fuck, Annette! You scared the shit out of me. You shouldn't sneak up on people like that!" I say as I try to stand up without losing my cigarette.

"I'm sorry, Ruby. I really didn't mean to bother you. I followed you out here and just wanted to see what you were doing out here in the dark, all by yourself."

Her tone is sweet and truthful.

"What does it look like I'm doing? I'm escaping fucking Jonestown in there," I reply.

She laughs at this comment as if she understands it could actually be true. We drink the Kool-Aid.

"Do you have another one?" she asks as she points to my cigarette. "Or maybe I can just have a drag off yours?"

"Sure," I concede.

She reaches to take the cigarette, except instead of removing it from my hand, she takes my hand and gently places it on her breast.

"You know, I was thinking 'bout what you said earlier and all, 'bout being next. I'm okay with that. I mean, only if you are."

She presses my hand forcefully under her shirt and starts kissing me, starting with my cheeks and then aggressively making her way to my mouth. She pauses and looks into my eyes.

"What do you say?" she whispers.

"I do like a challenge," I murmur back as I slip my other hand under her skirt and follow my own path that leads well underneath her panties.

I am officially a certified lesbian, and after tonight, so is Annette Davis. And just like that, Slideshow Wednesdays have become my favorite day of the week, because if truth be told, being a good pussy-finger-diving lesbian requires Olympic training of epic proportions, and I just won the gold.

Chapter 7

TWO BY TWO

It is early Sunday morning. There is a dependable and safe comfort to a Sunday morning routine in my home. Sundays are the truest day of the Pentecost. It is a day of ritual—a day that holds constant reverence yet is guided by numerous rules, regulations, and ceremonies.

I awaken at our expected time to prepare for Sunday service. I hesitate to enter the kitchen for breakfast, as I hear my parents whispering fiercely to each other. I make grave efforts to not be discovered.

"He has called twice. Twice! And a collect call at that! Does he think we are made of money?"

Daddy speaks harshly to Momma, who is seated at the breakfast table, staring blankly into her black coffee. However, Daddy is not seated. He is pacing from one end of the room to the other, something I have never witnessed. As he paces, he runs his fingers through his hair that is not really there.

"I understand. I will take care of it, Larry. But it's Kevin. Larry, he is my brother. What do you expect me to do? He needs us. He needs me. He is completely alone, and he is alone in Israel for that matter. Israel. He just needs help to come home," Momma says as she tries to calm Daddy.

"Susan, do you hear yourself right now? Just listen to what you are saying. Your brother claims to have physically found Noah's Ark and is expecting us to fly him home. With the Ark, Susan. Not just any ark, THE Ark.

"He is not asking for us to fly him home, bring his luggage or some random piece of furniture. Noah's Ark, Susan. What on earth is he thinking? And why does your entire family continue to ignore the fact that he is completely and utterly insane?"

"Larry, don't say that! Please just take a minute and calm down. You are getting yourself all worked up over…"

Momma makes an attempt to take control of this unfortunate conversation, but to no avail.

"I've already had to deal with his excavation of the Holy Grail! Or did you forget, Susan?"

"No, I did not forget, Larry. How can I forget when you constantly bring it up every time my family needs me? And I will kindly ask you to watch your tone with me, Larry Joe Clancy," Momma says, although her tone is the one that needs watching.

I press my body against the wall, holding my breath. I've never heard Daddy talk this way to anyone, much less Momma. Daddy is always so soft-spoken and mild-tempered. To hear him speak to Momma in this tone makes me queasy.

"Remember when he dug up the Holy Grail with a shovel, Susie? A simple Walmart shovel. Do you? And then he said he couldn't touch it because he thought God would strike him dead. Do you remember? We sent him three hundred dollars so he could pay a bunch of homeless Christian Egyptians to help him bury it again. Do you remember?"

Daddy's tone is becoming alarmingly elevated, and his face is turning three shades of angry red.

"And what did I do for your family? Did I say no? Did I? Did I question you? No, no, I did not! I sent him the money. What the heck is wrong with your family? Kevin is just flat-out crazy, just like

WEEDS THROUGH THE FLOORBOARDS

your mother!" Daddy screams as he grabs his jacket and slams the door as he leaves.

It is eerily quiet. I peer around the corner, and I wait cautiously to observe Momma's next move. She stares blankly out the window and rubs her temples as if trying to release what has just happened.

"Good morning, Momma," I say, attempting to break the uncomfortable silence.

"Good morning," she barely responds. "You know what, baby girl? Your momma is feeling just a tad bit under the weather today. I think we will rest here at home. Would that be okay with you?"

"Of course, Momma. Whatever you need. Can I get you anything?" I ask nervously.

She doesn't respond. She speaks no words. She rises up from her chair and flows past me like I am not even there. She walks down the hall to her bedroom, where she quietly closes the door.

This is the first time that I can recall that she has ever missed church. Ever. This is not our routine. I am worried. I am panicked. I am distraught. I need her to tell me everything will be okay, but there is nothing but silence. When you have secrets, you have silence.

I quietly walk back to my bedroom and relive what I have just witnessed for the first time—a Holiday Inn Express moment. No one has asked me, but in my opinion, someone needs to take the wheels off Uncle Kevin's Holiday Inn Express trailer.

Chapter 8

THE PRICE IS RIGHT

We spend the next Saturday in front of the Dairy Barn on Fourth Street, waving flimsy white poster board signs reading, "Free Car Wash. Honk For Salvation." No one honks. They're all going to hell.

Arvil Barrett, the owner of Dairy Barn, sporadically allows us to use the water spigot on the side of the Dairy Barn and his parking lot to wash cars for Christ. I figure it's because Arvil Barrett is a flat-out pedophile wannabe who drinks Ernest and Julio Gallo out of a Styrofoam cup all day and looks at little boys in the parking lot.

Slideshow Wednesdays have ingrained in our God brains countless images of poor little Nicaraguan children in tattered clothes, squatting in the dirt, wearing no shoes, and smiling sheepishly for the camera. Today, we are raising money to send to the dirty Nicaraguan children—dirty meaning physically and spiritually.

But I'm not stupid. I don't believe for one minute that an occasional coin and some wadded-up old bills thrown into a plastic milk jug that's been cut in half can add up to any amount of money to aid poor orphans in an entirely different country.

It's like watching those St. Jude's commercials that have bald kids with cancer staring into a camera with one tear brimming from an eye as they give you literally thirty minutes to call in and miraculously save all the children.

Don't get me wrong. It's not that I am against scrubbing cars for Christ to help save the poor, lost souls of the children in Nicaragua. I can be a fucking St. Jude. But I would like to balance this charitable cause by contributing that I am also smoking enough weed to financially support the entire Sandinista revolution in Nicaragua. It's a win-win.

I am finishing drying the windshield of a Chevy Impala when I hear an actual honk for salvation. I turn to see Dewayne Mitchell pulling into the parking lot while waving his hand out the window. He slowly pulls right next to me.

"Hey there, Ruby. Where you been? I drove by the rock quarry all week. I waited for you after school, but you never showed. You just disappeared."

We awkwardly struggle to talk to each other like innocent, casual strangers, but in real life, Dewayne and I play Romp and Stomp and Cum and Go in the back of his Camaro most afternoons after school—except Wednesdays. Slideshow Wednesdays are reserved for Annette, who at this exact moment is shooting jealous, firelit glances at me and Dewayne from the other side of the parking lot.

"I already told you, Dewayne. My momma is having all sorts of fits and asking all kinda questions when I come home. I just need some time to get things settled."

It is hard to talk to Dewayne when I physically can feel Annette's darts shoot into my chest. I also feel the congregation's daggers as they all cease their activity to access my current situation, where I am engaged in a conversation not only with a boy, but also a boy of color. Coloreds are not allowed into the Kingdom, just like lesbians.

"Ruby!" Annette calls from across the parking lot.

Then there is silence. I wait to hear the cause for her emergency summons. But sometimes, silence says more than words.

Here I am. What a situation I have landed myself in. I am standing in the Dairy Barn parking lot with both of my lovers sparring over my attention. I look at Dewayne and then back at Annette. This current unfortunate circumstance I've landed into reminds me of the buffet at the Western Sizzlin'—too many choices and things of all colors and tastes.

The silence is broken as Momma peels into the parking lot in our brown LTD and yells frantically through the window.

"Ruby, come on now. We gotta go!"

There is an uncomfortable urgency in her voice. I, however, am most grateful for this interruption, although I am unclear as to what could be more important than cleaning cars for Christ.

I don't hesitate. I welcome the rescue. I jump into the car, where I barely pull my feet in the door before Momma skids out of the parking lot.

"Lord, child, your Aunt Dixie done got herself into another heap of mess. We gotta go get her."

This is not an unfamiliar field trip to me. Momma's eyes are red and puffy. I can tell she's been crying again. Between Noah's Ark, the Holy Grail, Daddy's fussing, Dark Dewayne, Same-Sex Annette, and now Dixie? I think Momma may need her very own Holiday Inn Express trailer soon.

*****

The Yell County Courthouse is the tallest building in all of Yell County. It has five floors and large white pillars in the front that remind me of pictures of the White House I see on PBS. Momma suspiciously parks the car in the very back, a for sure way to remain completely unseen. I am familiar with being unseen.

As we enter the large glass doors, Momma rushes straight up to the tiny window at the front of the lobby. The window is guarded by a lady with long blonde hair and bright-red lipstick. Her smile is soft and inviting as she slowly slides the window open. She looks like she should be one of those pretty models who elegantly display showcases on *The Price Is Right*. I love that show.

"Good afternoon. How can I help you today?" she asks politely.

"Dixie, please."

WEEDS THROUGH THE FLOORBOARDS

There is no need to offer any further information. Everyone in the Yell County legal system knows all about my infamous Aunt Dixie Anne Thomas.

"One second," Ms. Price Is Right says as she ruffles through all kinds of different-colored papers.

She licks the tip of her finger to separate all the pages.

"Here it is," she says as she slides one of the papers across the ledge to Momma. "How will you be paying today?" Ms. Price Is Right asks.

"How much is it?" Momma asks.

I would like to suggest that we make a bid, just like they do on *The Price Is Right*.

"Three hundred forty-eight dollars, please."

Damn. That's a solid forty-eight dollars more than Uncle Kevin's Holy Grail expedition. I look up at Momma's face just to verify that she is as shocked as I am. But Momma holds her composure, takes in a deep breath, and calmly digs through her purse, pulling out a mint-green credit card. I can see her hand quivering as she slides the card to Ms. Price Is Right.

"Give us a few minutes to get her processed. You can have a seat in—"

"I know, I know," Momma interrupts impatiently and turns to be seated on the bench directly behind us.

We are the only ones in the waiting room. It feels isolated and solitary.

Momma finally breaks the uncomfortable silence, saying, "Don't slouch, Ruby Jane. You know how bad that is for your posture. And there's no need to tell your daddy about what happened here today. You hear me?"

Her tone is harsh and untrusting.

"I won't, Momma," I reply.

I am good at keeping secrets.

The doors swing open in full force, and Dixie Anne Thomas walks out balls to the wall, straightening her skirt and attempting to brush her hair with her fingers. She looks stunning and beautiful. Only Dixie Anne Thomas can spend an entire night in a jail cell and exit looking like one of them models in the JCPenney Christmas catalog.

"Oh, sweet Jesus, Susie Q! You have no idea what I've been through! I swear, this place is the devil. The devil, I tell you! I was framed, and I didn't do shit!"

Dixie is the only human who can call Momma Susie Q and get away with it. She is also the only human in Yell County who is consistently framed and didn't do shit.

Momma says nothing and turns to walk out of the door. But if her face could talk? I would imagine all sorts of anger exploding. Dixie and I follow her out, remaining silent as well. Momma's silence makes us both nervous.

We all get into the LTD.

As soon as the doors shut, Momma turns to Dixie in the back seat and says, "Don't say another word. Not a word. You better get your life together, Dixie. Me and Larry? We just can't keep rescuing you every time you don't do shit."

She includes air quotes at the end.

"Rescuing me? Is that what you think you are doing, Susie? Let's be clear. I am not an abandoned dog at a goddamn shelter. I do not need rescuing from anyone! How dare you lecture me! You? You, Susie, of all people?"

Momma quickly glances my way. She almost looks afraid, like Dixie is about to reveal something to me that I shouldn't know.

Secrets.

Momma starts the car and leaves the parking lot to take Dixie home. The drive is unnerving and quiet. I want to say something, anything, to break this awful tension. I imagine blurting out, "I'm fucking a black man with a huge dick and a white girl with a small pussy!" That would surely break the silence.

Finally, Dixie offers the truce.

"All right, all right. I'm sorry," she says as she tries to close the can of worms she just opened. "Listen, Susie."

Her tone is now soft and almost childlike.

WEEDS THROUGH THE FLOORBOARDS

"I really am trying. I know you don't think I am trying to change, but I really am. I just applied for a new job down at The Mill. Roy Dell, the manager, says I'd be a real good fit."

Don't be confused. The Mill is not an actual working mill. The Mill is a bar of extremely questionable tenants and ex-convicts who camp out all day, drink copious amounts of beer and colored drinks with cherries in them, and snort so many lines of coke they could accurately chalk the entire football field at the Western Yell County High School.

"Oh, and me and Bobby?" Dixie adds, further attempting her convincing.

"What about you and Bobby? Dixie, you know he ain't nothing but trouble. I don't have anything good to say about him."

"Well, we are finally gonna get married."

"Dixie, you cannot be serious. How many times do we have to talk about this? Please tell me you are not considering this option."

Momma is riled up at this point and ready to rumble.

Bobby Ray Montgomery used to be a mechanic down at the Rev an' Roll, but he lost his job on account of his last vacation, which was an extended stay in jail. Bobby Ray and Dixie are two forms of toxic when they get together. Their relationship reminds me of those multiple-choice questions in my science class.

Question: What are some characteristics you would consider when choosing a boyfriend?

A. A drunk
B. A deadbeat
C. A violent deadbeat
D. A drug addict
E. All of the above

Dixie has chosen E.

"Well, regardless of your complete and total lack of enthusiasm for my upcoming day, I do hope you all can make it to the wedding. It's gonna be something real special, I tell ya."

"Dixie, you and I will entertain this conversation without Ruby Jane. This is not appropriate to speak of in front of her, and you and I both know why."

I wish I knew why. Secrets.

"And if you do marry him? Why on blessed earth would you do it in a Catholic church? Of all places! The Holy Rosary? Why? Help me understand!"

Momma is almost shouting now. I can see the veins bulging on her neck.

"You know why, Susie! Quit acting like you are better than me. Bobby and I are getting married, and it's that simple. You know I have to do this, and you know why. This conversation is over!"

I genuinely thank God that we are finally pulling into the Lamplighter Trailer parking lot. This needs an ending.

"You're damn right it's over, 'cause I ain't got nothing else to say to you!" she screams back as she slams the door so hard, I think the windows will shatter.

But that doesn't actually occur, because Dixie dramatically turns around and adds "Oh, and thank you so much for rescuing me," as she pathetically howls and barks like a dog.

All the while, she is smiling at me, raising her hand to mimic a phone to her ear and mouthing "Call me" as she sashays her ass from side to side and confidently walks up the stairs to her trailer.

This family and their fucking trailers. FUCK!

*****

Brother Eddie and Annette's parents are going on a ten-day missionary trip to El Salvador to recruit sinners and save lost souls from eternal damnation. I find this most interesting, because I am almost certain not one of them can locate El Salvador on a *Merriam-Webster's Student Atlas*. And because it happens to be during the school year, they've asked my parents if Annette can stay with us while they are gone.

Annette and I spend the entirety of our days learning religious stuff and our evenings learning bed stuff. Annette is perfect. She

WEEDS THROUGH THE FLOORBOARDS

knows how to love me, and we slowly learn how to love each other. When she kisses me, I pretend I am at our wedding. She raises my veil, and Brother Eddie says, "You may now kiss the bride." And the organ music blares the traditional wedding march.

It is during these intimate moments that I realize I will never have this experience. I will never marry Annette. I will never marry at all. I will never be happy. I will never be allowed. We are not allowed in the Kingdom.

One night during Annette's stay, I decide to tell her how much I love her, how much I need her and adore her and want to spend the rest of my life with her. I want to tell her everything. No more secrets.

We are in the backyard, catching fireflies in Momma's now inherited Jesus Saves Garden. Momma has given us each a Mason jar with tiny pinholes poked on top of the metal lids.

"Netti, do you think we'd be together someday? I mean, really be together?" I ask her.

She is gracefully kneeling next to the rosebush, where she is attempting to collect the brightest firefly I have ever seen in my entire life. I am convinced that this is a sign.

"Of course, Ruby. I love you. I love you with all I have in me. I love your soul and your smile, and I love your heart. I will give you everything I can. I promise to always be here," she says, and her sweet smile literally makes my heart shiver on my insides. "I will never leave. Never."

I feel a small tear in my eye as I realize that I have found someone as sweet and loving as Annette.

"And, Ruby, if you ever fuck Dewayne Mitchell again, I will literally cut your tits off and shove them down your throat," she says as she calmly takes the firefly between her fingers, squishes it, places it in her mouth, swallows it, and walks away.

I have never considered myself to be a world scholar by any means, but I am smart enough to know that this is probably not a good time to tell her I think I am pregnant.

Chapter 9

MY CROSS TO BEAR

I am sick. I am actually sicker than sick. I throw up every morning, every afternoon, and every time an aroma approaches my nostrils. I have skipped my period.

After the unfortunate Firefly Murder Incident, I decide it is in my best interest to not share any of this information with Annette. As a lesbian, I really enjoy the pleasure she brings my tits; and rest assured, I plan on keeping them. Dixie clearly becomes my one and only option. I have no one else in my life.

I call her the next afternoon and ask her to pick me up after school, something I have never done in my entire life. I tell Momma that we are going to pick peaches in the orchard on Skyline. I see the circles of uncertainty swimming in Momma's I-Know-Everything-And-You-Are-Lying Brain. She is reluctant in her agreement but finally decides I can go.

Dixie picks me up in her ancient, archaic station wagon. I am not at all impressed that she is on the dot, right on time. I am, however, impressed that the wheels are still attached to this car. It reminds me of one of those paint-by-numbers picture books I got for Christmas when I was five. Every few feet, it changes color.

Dixie skids into the parking lot, saddles blazing and blowing the horn repeatedly when she sees me sitting on the front steps to the school. She cannot be quiet and discreet to save her ass.

She leans over, kicking the passenger side open with her right leg.

"You gotta give it some umph and a bit of TLC to get it to cooperate!" she yells to me through the window.

The ashtray is overwhelmed with cigarette butts, ashes, and crumpled white paper straw covers. I am most confident that we could disappear for several months and not need a damn thing considering the wealth of random shit loaded in the back seat.

We drive mindlessly for several miles. Then she finally breaks our silence.

"Now what is this all about, Ruby?"

I cannot bring myself to speak the words into truth. Once these words come out, they become a real baby. I cannot bring myself to care enough to say the words. I cannot bring myself to be honest. Secrets.

"Well, what is it?" Dixie almost demands from me. "I know you didn't just call out of the blue to randomly drive around this godforsaken town. Are you in trouble? Do you need money?"

"No, it's nothing like that," I finally respond. "I...I just...I don't know, Dixie. I don't know what to do. There is just so much to tell you, and I can't...I can't tell anybody."

"Well, why not? For fuck's sake! What is wrong? It can't be that bad. Are you failing school? Did you miss a fucking Sunday school class? Oh, God forbid, you probably said a fucking cuss word, and now you need confession."

She laughs.

"Seriously, Ruby, I don't need this drama right now. I'm sure whatever it is, everything will be fine."

"I think I'm pregnant!" I shout out.

Dixie's face goes stone-solid blank. She takes a moment to marinate the words that I've just released into our lives.

"You are what?" she asks.

She is dazed, and rightfully so, as she appears to have been slapped in the face.

"What the fuck! Ruby! What the actual fuck!" she screams.

And then Dixie Anne Thomas tilts her head all the way back and begins laughing hysterically. She bellows a sound from her soul that is not only alarming but also frightening. I stare back at her in total disbelief. I am in shock. I am horrified. Why is she laughing at this unfathomable predicament? Who does that? Dixie Anne Thomas, that's who.

What on earth is wrong with her? Her fits get louder and louder with each second that passes. Maybe Momma has been right all along about Dixie sharing all the same genetics with Uncle Kevin when it comes to the Bat Shit Crazies.

When she finally catches her breath, she says, "Oh, sweet Ruby, I really am sorry about all that."

She literally dries the tears from her face.

"Who knew you had it in you? Go big or go home, right? Sweet baby Jesus. Are you sure, honey? Did you take a test? Oh, wait! Who did you…well, you know."

"No, I haven't taken a test. I don't have any money, and you of all people know, Dixie, that everyone in this town would tell Momma and Daddy and the entire congregation if I ever bought a pregnancy test. You can't do nothing in this shithole town without everyone knowing your business!"

"Well, you are right about that, sweet Ruby. You are certainly right. Well, this shithole town won't think one thing about Ms. Dixie Thomas buying a pregnancy test, that's for damn sure. Trust me, first step is to get that done. Now are you gonna spill the beans? Who is this young, interesting fella that has you knocked up? Oh, wait! Don't tell me. Let me guess."

Dixie is acting like we are both on a game show, and there's a prize between door number one, door number two, and door number three.

"Oh, wait! I know, I know, I know," she says, sounding almost giddy at this point. "It's Travis from your Sunday school class. I see how he looks at you, Ruby. Oh, wait, or is it that Raymond boy from Bible study? Huh? Spill it!"

"It's actually Dewayne. Dewayne Mitchell."

"Dewayne Mitchell?" she repeats to make certain she has heard correctly. "You mean black Dewayne Mitchell? Beula's boy?" she asks again, completely and utterly shocked.

"Yes," I respond as I try to assess what she is thinking.

"So what you are telling me is that you not only had sex, but you had sex and might be pregnant from a black man? Sweet mercy of Mary. A black man? You have been having sex with a black man. What the hell, Ruby!"

"But wait. There's more," I say, feeling like those annoying Ronco commercials, where you think it is over, and you hear, "But wait! There's more! Buy one, get one free!"

"Ruby, there can't be much more. What more could there possibly be?" she asks as if she is exhausted.

I hesitate, looking down so she cannot see my eyes. They are overwhelmed with tears.

"I'm also sleeping with Annette from church, and I love her. Dixie, I love her with everything in me. I want to marry her, just like you wanna marry Bobby."

Aunt Dixie bows her head deep down into the steering wheel, reaches for a Camel cigarette, takes a breath, looks dead square into my eyes, and says, "It's about goddamn time someone takes my place in this family."

*****

We slowly pull the station wagon into the Arco Drugstore parking lot in the City Mall down on Main Street. Dixie parks in the very back, as if we are hiding from the pregnancy police, who will approach us at any moment, shining a flashlight in our face and demanding we pee in a cup.

"Okay, now I'm gonna run in and get you a test. I want you to go to the front of the store and ask for a value pack of BIC lighters.

They always keep those in the back so you kids don't steal 'em. Keep them distracted, and I'm gonna snatch the pregnancy test. Got it?"

"What do you mean snatch? You are stealing it? What the actual hell, Dixie?" I asked.

"Not so much stealing it, Ruby. I am borrowing the monetary value of what the city owes me for keeping me locked up illegally on numerous occasions. They owe me," she replies, emphasizing the word *owe*. "And whatever you do, do not talk to anyone or bring attention to us. You got it?"

I nod my head. I feel like I am in the middle of *The Brady Bunch* episode where Greg steals the goat mascot from Westdale High. I love that show.

I walk into the Arco and straight up to the front, where there is an old lady with snow-white hair. Her skin is wrinkled like cracked desert crevices, and her eyes look like road maps. She has the name Berta on her red plastic name tag, which is haphazardly pinned to a dingy white lab coat. Berta looks like she died last year.

Berta looks at me and says, "Well, what do you need?"

She is irritated, and her voice sounds like she lives on cigarettes and all things smoky.

"Can I please have a value pack of BIC lighters?" I ask as my voice shakes.

I am scared, and I feel almost certain Berta is gonna call Momma and tell her what I am up to. I attempt my try at sounding innocent and make the inflection of my voice sound like a virgin proving her case before the sacrificial altar.

Berta leaves the front counter, shaking her head as she walks to the back of the store. I look behind me and see Dixie feverously shoving any and all things into her purse. Dear God, she looks like she is Christmas shopping for the needy children in El Salvador. What the fuck?

Berta returns to the counter, where she presents to me a multi-pack of blue BIC lighters.

"$2.78," she says.

At this point, Dixie grabs my arm and announces loudly to anyone who can hear, "I'm sorry. We have to leave. I'm not feeling well. Bye, Ms. Berta!"

And we both rush out of the store, hand in hand, and back to the car.

"Whew!"

She laughs as we both land back into the car. She proudly empties the fruits of her labor into her lap—three lipsticks, one Revlon Perfect Match Powder, two packs of Certs, two boxes of BC Powder, one unicorn keychain, one box of tampons, and one EPT pregnancy test in a square brown-and-yellow box.

"You stole all of that?" I ask in shock.

"You mean to tell me you ain't never stole anything in your life? It ain't stealing if it's owed to you," Dixie says. "They all owe me. And besides, I know what you're thinking. The Bible says thou shalt not steal. I'm pretty sure the Bible also says thou shalt not fuck women when you are a woman and at the same damn time get knocked up by a black man, and thou shalt not judge. But here you are, checking all the boxes."

I couldn't argue with that.

*****

We are sitting in Dixie's kitchen. It's actually a trailer combination of a kitchen slash living room. I like it here. It makes me feel safe. The bright linoleum floors have calming green-and-orange squares that are so eloquently combined with one pattern after another. Patterns make me feel stable. The curtains hanging above the kitchen sink feel like they want to change, but they are too old.

Dixie pours a Dr Pepper for me and a Coors for her.

"Now all you gotta do is drink this and wait. When you gotta pee, you go in the bathroom and pee on this stick. It's that simple."

Simple is not a word I even find comparable to what I am feeling.

While we wait, Dixie pulls out her Green Stamps coupon book and starts gluing in her stamps. There is an odd store in the middle of town where you can trade in your stamps for peculiar things, like ceramic ashtrays shaped like cats and crocheted covers for toilet lids.

"Ya know, you could really be something if you fixed up yourself a bit, Ruby. For the love of God, I don't know why your daddy insists you stay so fucking homely," she says, breaking our pregnancy pause. "Here. Come here and sit on the floor next to me."

I crouch on the floor with my back to her shins. She opens the box of stolen tampons and starts rolling them up in my hair, tying them with the little strings to my long strands.

"A little something I learned while locked up, sugar. Girl, you can use tampons for anything!"

I sit quietly and let her roll me up. I feel like a white Rastafarian.

"We'll just leave these in for a bit, and then presto! You will have bounce and wave to that flatness you wanna call hair."

I sit quietly, sipping my Dr Pepper and letting Dixie fold each of the cotton capsules into my long strands. It is at this exact moment I realize that a small portion of the left side of my hair is missing, a result of continuous and current-day twisting and Granddaddy Tuesdays.

I take a breath in and out, in and out. The pee gate has opened. I take the stick, walk into the bathroom, and balance myself on the toilet. I feel like I might faint. I pee on the stick and set it down on the bathroom counter, and then I wait.

While I wait, I evaluate my mophead of tampons in the mirror. I look fucking ridiculous.

Dixie screams from the living room, "Well, what is it? A bouncing baby boy? A twinkle-eyed girl? You're killing me out here."

I glance down on the counter. Blue lines are ever so cautiously bleeding throughout the window of the stick and making a formation.

Dixie impatiently pulls the door open and shouts, "What is it? Oh, for fuck's sake, Ruby!"

She grabs the stick off the counter, examines the results, and in an eerily calm tone says, "Humph, well, will you look at that, Ruby Jane, a perfect cross, just like Jesus."

*****

WEEDS THROUGH THE FLOORBOARDS

I utilize the prolonged and tiring days after my Jesus-On-The-Cross positive pregnancy results in deep contemplation as to what I will do. I daydream of packing my things like they do in Lifetime movies, tragically crying and pulling drawers from dressers, making no sense of what I shove into a suitcase.

I run far away to another city, where I give birth completely alone to a black baby I will name after his father and live happily ever after with Annette. I literally conduct intense research on cities in all of Mexico where society rejects can flee to and have a baby for free. I am off course and feel hopeless.

If I am not throwing up, I am lying for hours at a time in my bed, crying. I have no one. I imagine telling my mom the truth, only to be sent away to a Jesusy Reform Camp. I heard that Sarah Neils once got pregnant, and they sent her off to a Jesus in Charge Camp, which is one of those unwed teenage mother homes, and she took an entire bottle of sleeping pills she snuck in from her grandma's dresser. I would like to get Sarah's advice, but Sarah Neils is dead.

I am lying in my bed when Momma comes in the room.

"Ruby Jane, I need you to talk to me and tell me what on earth is wrong. You just haven't been yourself lately. I am really worried. This is not you! Remember what I've always told you. There ain't nothing you cannot tell me, baby girl. What is it?"

"It is nothing, Momma," I reply. "I just want to be left alone."

But Suzie Q. Clancy is not one who gives up easily.

"Are things okay at the church? Are you feeling sad…or depressed?"

I remain silent. Momma continues her interrogation.

"Are you having a hard time at school? Come on now. I can't pray for you if I don't know what I am praying for."

"It's really nothing. I just don't feel well, and I have a lot going on right now, Momma. Don't take things so personally," I answer, hoping this will immediately end this difficult conversation.

Realizing that I am not going to submit to her inquiry, Momma gets up from the bed, silently tidies up my room by folding a blanket I have tossed to the floor, and putting my used towel in the laundry

47

basket. She then turns and looks at me once more before leaving the room.

Later that evening, I emerge from my cave and walk silently to the kitchen and attempt to put something in my stomach. I can hear *Family Feud* playing on the TV and Momma and Daddy both shouting out answers, each one trying to outdo the other.

I am pulling the Apple Jacks from the counter when my eyes fixate on a small postcard with a beautiful picture of a white-sand beach and emerald-green water. Curious, I turn the postcard over; and carefully scripted in blue ink on the back, it reads:

> Dear Susie,
>
> It is with the utmost pride that I announce the arrival of my first child. Francis and I are finally expecting our very much prayed for bundle of joy. However, due to the fact that we both conceived this miracle from God in Jamaica, we felt it was important to let our families know that the child will be black when he is born. Francis is doing well.
>
> Love in our Christ and Lord Jesus Savior,
> Kevin

At this moment, I realize that Aunt Francis and I finally have something in common and that no one bothered to take the wheels off Uncle Kevin's trailer.

Chapter 10

THE ART OF
SWAN DIVING

When I come home from school the very next day, I find Momma waiting for me at the kitchen table. This is something that she has never done before. She is alone. Her face is unpredictable, yet her eyes are angry.

"Sit down," she says calmly.

I am not sure how to address this command from a mother who rarely places instructions into words.

"I found a marijuana cigarette today in your closet."

She gently places the joint on the table for me to see.

"I need you to explain to me what is really going on, Ruby Jane."

She does not even allow me to gather my thoughts. My immediate thought is to not panic and to throw out a believable lie. However, my actual thought process is only able to focus on the absurdity of the statement at hand. Who the fuck actually calls a joint a marijuana cigarette? I find it hard to not correct her lack of knowledge on drug use vocabulary.

There are no words being spoken. I am not sure how much time passes before Momma finally shatters the uncomfortable silence.

"Your daddy and I cannot and will not continue to support your disrespect of God and your church elders. You think we don't know things, Ruby Jane? But we do know things."

We just don't talk about them is what I want to say. This is proving to be a compelling evaluation of my life's work considering that only eleven months ago, I fucked the last teen revival preacher, who came to spread the Word of the great God Almighty and ended up forcing me to spread my legs in the back of his Cadillac down at the old Lock and Dam.

"You are leaving today," Momma says firmly.

"Leaving today for where? What do you mean?" I ask.

"You are going to Bridges for Christ, where you will stay until you decide that your reckless choice of drugs and the choices you are making about your life here, well, this is not the way of Jesus Christ, our Lord and Savior.

"This path you are currently on? This destructive path you are walking? It is dangerous, Ruby, and there will be a moment when God won't allow you to ever return. Is that what you want? I have never been more disappointed in your choices, Ruby!"

Did she just say choices? My choices?

"Momma, what path are you talking about? If I am on a path, no one told me about it. I didn't see any signs along the way directing me anywhere!"

My voice is shaking.

"The path of sin and total abomination! You are clearly doing drugs. And don't think we are all oblivious to this...this so-called inappropriate friendship you have up and started with Beula's boy."

Her tone sounds like those words feel like dirt in her mouth.

"It's just flat-out disgraceful! It is disgraceful to not only us but to the Kingdom and our entire congregation. And people talk, Ruby. They talk about you and...and...and...well, you and other girls."

Momma almost whispers this, clearly to make sure no one can hear these words come into the universe.

"They say things that are so horrible. I...we will not stand for it."

These words sound more like a prepared sermon and less like a concerned mother who worries about her child.

"Well, maybe that's the problem, Momma," I begin to retaliate. "This so-called path y'all keep harking on? Maybe it's not my path. It's your path, the Kingdom's path, but I don't belong on this fucking path!" I scream.

And as expected, her hand, known only for its gentleness, lands firmly across my face, the blow sending me into the realization that I most likely deserve it.

"Get your things and get in the car."

She walks away without as much as a look back.

On a positive note, I am actually a bit excited to practice my Lifetime movie packing skills, where I am overwhelmed and in a fit of rage. I pull whatever is accessible and furiously slam it into a bag that may or may not hold a pack of Marlboro Lights, a fifth of Jack Daniel's, an impressionable bump of coke, and a solid quarter bag of some badass weed.

Even my suitcase requires a Holiday Inn Express trailer.

*****

We pull into the desolate circular drive of the Bridges for Christ Rehab Center. It is now pitch-black outside, an appropriate match to the current color of my soul. As I cautiously enter the lobby, it smells of green Listerine and old wax candles. It is clear that I do not belong here. It is clear that I do not belong anywhere.

Momma hesitantly takes my arm by the elbow and walks me rather forcefully to the top of the stairs.

"Go," she demands and points her finger down an empty hallway.

"Momma, please don't leave me here. Please..."

My childish begging does nothing to persuade Momma that I belong to a different deck of cards than what I have been dealt the day she brought me into this world. And in one moment, she is gone, and I am completely alone.

An elderly man standing well more than six feet tall approaches me from behind an oval desk and places his hand delicately on my shoulder. He squeezes my shoulder like he is checking the firmness of melons in the summer.

"Hello, Ruby, and welcome. My name is Dr. Broach. I will be your guide as we decide together how to place you back into God's forever, infinite, and holy graces and loving arms of salvation. Now let's get you settled. Do you have any questions?"

"Yes, sir," I quietly respond. "Y'all got any trailers around here?"

*****

My room is located at the very end of the hallway. It is completely dark and cold, and there is nothing contained there except an old dresser with faded silver knobs, a small twin bed smothered against a sterile concrete wall, and a fluorescent light that flickers an uncertain pathway into a small bathroom. There are no mirrors. There are no locks. There are no hopes.

I take a moment, and my mind wanders and reflects as to why I am really here. My left hand naturally travels up to the left portion of my hair, and I wrap a strand so tight around my finger, I feel the roots separating from my scalp, just like I am separated from everything in my life that means the most. I don't have Momma or Daddy. I don't have Aunt Dixie. I don't have Netti.

Oh my god, Netti! Does she even know I am here? Will she think I have left her? Will she come and visit? Can I even have visitors? I have no way to reach her.

I place my Lifetime movie packing suitcase at the end of the bed, and I breathe into my lungs the absolute feeling of despair. I lay my head onto the starch white pillow, lift my entire body onto the bed, and attempt to stop the tears that have welled up in my eyes and are awaiting to fall.

"Well, well, well. Would you look at this?"

WEEDS THROUGH THE FLOORBOARDS

Shocked, I jump from my stance on the bed, realizing someone is actually sitting in complete darkness against the wall opposite my bed. Heart pounding, I make an effort toward the bathroom light. But before I can reach it, the voice continues with an eerie, melodic rendition of a song.

"You can check out anytime you like, but you can never leave."

This is followed by one of the most sensual, enticing female voices I have ever heard in my life.

"I'm Betty. I'm thirty-two and addicted to meth about as much as I'm addicted to women. This here?"

She uses her stretched-out palm to circle the entire room.

"This place right here is your run-of-the-mill, top-shelf, pray-the-gay-away, drown-the-drugs, solicit-for-salvation, last-stop-on-the-train center for troubled souls. Welcome, my friend."

"Hi. I am, well, I'm Ruby," I reply sheepishly.

"Ruby, huh?" she says. "Ruby is a gem, the most sinful color of all, but I suppose you know that seeing as how you are here and all. Please allow me the honor of being your personal cruise director on the Seas of the Unhinged."

She slides close to me on the mattress. It is unnerving. Her mouth is now very close to my ear, and she licks her lips.

"This place here? This place will shut you completely up, drive you completely down, and leave you completely empty. It sucks the sinful soul right out of you. But hey, here we are. Would you look at us, already fast friends. And do you know what real friends do, Ruby Gem? Real friends support each other no matter what. And do you know how we do that, Ruby Gem?"

At this point, I have no idea where this unexpected conversation is headed.

"I'm really not sure, but I guess I am willing to support you… whatever that means," I reply to her question.

"That's wonderful news. I really like you already. But hey, I like women period. Now what do you say? Shall we simply cut to the chase? We both know why we were sent here. No need to pussyfoot around. Ah, speaking of pussy, you want to get stoned or just go straight to the fucking part?"

Her small, soft palm opens wide to display a kaleidoscope of multicolored pills—dark pink, light pink, baby blue, white, and white with blue. I cannot remember the last time I smiled this big.

"Go big or go home," I say.

"Oh, I do like you, Ruby Gem, my Ruby Gem. You better buckle the fuck up, buttercup, because we are about to go for a ride."

And just like that, my stay at the Bridges for Christ Rehab Center gets balls-to-the-wall better.

*****

Her name is Betty Mason. She is fifteen years older than me, fifteen inches wider than me, and is overwhelmingly overflowing with countless excuses for a variety of logical reasons why we should stay in this godforsaken, cultish, suffocating, soul-crushing reform center.

Truth be told, I do find Betty to be most helpful during my involuntary confinement. Betty has the best weed I've ever smoked. She has the softest hair I've ever touched. She has the bluest eyes I've ever looked into. She has the best ass I've ever fucked. She has the funniest laugh I've ever heard. She is graciously more than willing to entertain not only the lips on my mouth but also the lips between my legs.

We spend our entire days in therapy and then more therapy and then therapy about therapy, and then we do another therapy about the therapy we've had before. We sit through countless sermons of how we must reform or risk damnation in the eternal lake of fire. We are reminded of how the Tribulation is right around the corner, and the dead in Christ shall rise when the roll is called up yonder.

We hear how smoking, drinking, sexual deviances, and homosexuality will lead to our impending and immediate spiritual death and our inability to be with loved ones after the Tribulation, where we will all be left alone with Satan. We are already alone. Honestly, do I really want to even live at this point under the duress of such rules?

Betty and I spend our evenings like undercover lovers, sneaking in and out of each other's rooms, although we have convinced

Brother Lewis and Dr. Broach that we would both excel in the reformation process and be more apt to support each other if we are able to room together.

Brother Lewis, the head God counselor, concedes this to be a fabulous idea and is grateful for our insight and willingness to do the much-needed work for this cause. What better mentor for me than an elder woman who can assist in molding and shaping me into the woman my Christ family wishes me to be?

Betty and I spend countless hours in fictitious, religious therapeutic art class, learning how to manage our addictions to copious amounts of drugs and, quite frankly, to each other. We crisscross applesauce bright-colored fabric into organic bullshit kitchen pot holders to pacify our intense desire to be together at all times. We say what they want to hear and hear what they want to say.

On my fifteenth day on the Bridges for Christ Rehab Tour, Betty Mason furiously rummages through my Lifetime movie clothes drawer, affectionately and mindfully choosing a few of my favorite winter scarves and my absolute all-time go-to pair of red leggings, which I am forbidden to wear in public. She ties them around her neck and jumps from the cafeteria balcony—with the scarves still attached around her neck, might I add. She sure does know how to dress for success.

Go big or go home.

Chapter 11

T-MINUS SEVEN MONTHS

Upon learning of Betty's suicide, Momma promptly retrieves me from my Cult Sabbatical Rehab Efforts. I assume that one would think I am now in contemplation of scarf swan diving. However, I am simply envious. I am actually jealous, because I am still here, indifferent to others' feelings about swan diving, I suppose.

I cautiously drift back into my mundane, black-baby-carrying lesbian life as if nothing ever happened. I arrive back home on a Tuesday.

After I unpack my Lifetime movie suitcase, I walk into our backyard. The sun is brilliantly shining, and I can feel the warmth embracing my body. It is a comfort that I am longing for today. I lay my entire body down on the soft grass, peering up at the sky. I contemplate.

I wonder if Betty is there or if Betty is here. Can she see me? Is she free? I can smell her hair and the lavender Jergens lotion from her skin and taste the cherry ChapStick from her inviting lips. I can physically feel her arms wrap around me and her tongue trace the corners of my mouth.

The dam of pity breaks. I sob. I sob for her and for me. I sob for everything I feel and even more for what I cannot feel. And then there is silence.

As I open my eyes, there, just to my left, lies a group of weeds growing and flourishing among the valiant, colorful green grass. Weeds are so resilient. You can't kill weeds, because they are already dead.

*****

Life returns to what I have come to feel as normal. I return to Annette. I return to Slideshow Wednesdays. I return to school, only to realize no one even noticed my departure. I am never seen.

I do, however, feel like I am seen in PE, because I am the only one wearing a long dress as opposed to the required, school-issued uniform shorts. I am also not allowed to participate in our square dancing lessons this week, because Daddy has refused to sign my permission slip.

On this particular day, Coach Lee is making us all run bleachers. I don't mind so much. I like the thrill of my heart beating hard in my chest. It helps me remember I am alive.

"Do you think you can help me sometime with my English paper?" Charlotte Miers asks while we are bent over, trying to catch our breath. "I read your essay from last month, and I think you are a really good writer, Ruby."

No one is more shocked to hear this than me. I have never spoken to Charlotte Miers a day in my life. She is nothing more than a stuck-up bitch whose family moved to Yell County two years ago. Everyone knows her daddy makes his money by cheating good and honest people. They live in an enormous house on Skyline Drive, which includes a horse barn and a garage for more than one car.

I don't hate her. I just don't like her much. However, she isn't fuck-ugly, which means I would actually fuck her if the chance presents itself.

"Sure," I reply with utter and complete lack of enthusiasm. "I suppose that will be okay. I mean, I really don't know how I can help much."

"Your last paper was amazing! I loved your word choice and the way you used figurative language. Very impressive. I want to learn how to be a better writer."

Whatever, bitch. I want to learn how to be a better whore. I have goals too.

"Well, I will have my mom call your mom, and maybe we can…"

Charlotte is still speaking when I begin to lose my balance. The entire gym starts to swallow me and sways my existence from left to right to left. Everything is in slow motion as I attempt to stay standing, but my body will not allow it. I drop dead on the hard floor.

When I finally open my eyes, Coach Lee is shouting down to me, and all the girls in gym class are staring at me and whispering back and forth.

"Can you hear me, Ruby? Someone call 911!" Coach Lee screams across the gym. "Just stay still, Ruby. Everything's gonna be fine. No need to worry."

But that is not exactly true. There is absolutely a reason to worry. I feel something, a sensation that spreads from my back to my lower legs. I then feel a warm liquid slowly fan out onto the left palm of my hand.

When I lift my hand up to my eyes, it is completely covered in the most brilliant shade of red I've ever seen, an astonishingly similar shade to the leggings Betty used to swan dive from her life.

I cannot explain what happens next. I am literally lying on the gym floor with bright-red blood seeping out of my body. And for some incredibly inexplicable reason, my very first thought is that it is Valentine's Day. I am actually going to bleed to death and die on Valentine's Day. What a blessing.

*****

The door to my hospital room slowly opens, and Momma leans her head in and whispers, "Can I come in, Ruby Jane?"

She doesn't wait for me to answer. She enters and quietly closes the door behind her, walks to the edge of my hospital bed, and sits down. She uses her fingers to straighten her hair, as well as smooth the lines on her denim skirt.

"We both know what happened, Ruby," she says.

But do we? Do we really know, or are we just pretending we know?

She continues.

"The doctor says that...he...he says that...well, he says that everything will heal in its own time."

Oh, did he now? I sarcastically say in my head. Nothing ever heals in its own time. Even I know that.

"He also says that you can come home tomorrow morning if, well, if you rest and all the lab results come back normal. Until then, I am going to head home. You know your daddy. He needs his supper."

"Momma, Dixie knows. I told her when—" I say.

"Shhh," she says, cutting me off.

Momma gets up, walks slowly to me, and tenderly kisses the top of my hair. I cannot explain what this moment feels like. I am in a state of shock. Momma knows. She knows about the baby, yet she is calm. She is loving and supportive. I feel a warmth envelop my bones.

I am embarrassed for thinking that Momma won't understand my predicament. I am experiencing for the first time that I am about to discover a real truth with my family. I am on the edge of telling truths and being accepted for all the truths that I am, for all the truths that I have already been, and for all the truths I have not been allowed to be. I have never felt happier. Finally, I have hope.

Momma turns to leave and says, "And, Ruby Jane? Let's be up front and crystal clear about all of this. Don't ever speak of this again."

Did she say again? It still has not been spoken of. I'm confused.

"Do you hear me, child? Never. This didn't happen, none of it. I will deal with what to tell your father and others. But this?"

She is pointing her finger and making a circular motion around the room as if trying to capture it all into one space.

"This. Did. Not. Happen. And if I ever find out who put you in this condition? I swear to God in heaven and in all his glory, I will personally call Uncle Kevin and have him bury that son of a bitch in the same hole he dug for the Ark."

And with that, she gracefully leaves the hospital room.

I am stunned. I sit in complete silence, twisting the plastic hospital band around my wrist. I wonder what Uncle Kevin would think if he knew I spilled Momma's black grandbaby out on a gymnasium floor on Valentine's Day. Somehow, I think Uncle Kevin and Andy Gibb Jesus would be Team Ruby.

Chapter 12

AN UNFORTUNATE INCIDENT ON THE WAY TO PIGGLY WIGGLY

I t is exactly two days before Dixie's anxiously awaited nuptials at the Holy Rosary Catholic Church. Dixie picks me up from school six days after I am released from the That-Never-Happened Hospital.

I am secretly hoping we are headed off to another one of Dixie's They-Owe-Me, Free-For-All Shoplifting Extravaganzas. Currently, I am in need of four winter scarves and one pair of bright-red leggings that unfortunately were lost in the Betty Swan Dive incident.

"Hey, baby girl," Dixie happily greets me with a lit cigarette the length of the California coast hanging from her lips. "How ya doing?"

She awkwardly reaches across the seat, wraps her arms around me, and makes an attempt to hug every emotion away. Her effort is successful. It is at this moment that I wish Dixie were my very own momma.

"Your momma told me what happened, Ruby. I ain't real sure what to say. I just…I just think sometimes things happen for a reason, and sometimes, it really is for the best. I know that sounds like cliché bullshit, but in this case, the problem solved itself."

Yeah, it solved itself all over the gymnasium floor.

"Your momma, on the other hand," she continues as she applies bright-pink lip gloss while primping in the rearview mirror, "is not speaking to me right now on account of me knowing first and not telling her. Ya know, I just don't get her."

She places the gloss back into her purse and rubs her lips together.

"This is not a fucking competition."

She looks directly at me.

"She has always been…well…I don't know. She's just been… she's just been jealous of me."

"Jealous of you? Why?" I ask.

"Because I do whatever the fuck I want to do. I don't worry nothing about what people think of me. Now you know I love your momma. I would do anything in the world for that woman. She's my sister. We are blood. But sometimes, she is the most self-righteous bitch I've ever met. Always turning her nose up to me. Thinking she's better than me. She thinks I am nothing more than unsaved white trash on a nosedive to hell."

I am not sure how to respond to this. The harsh words directed toward Momma make me uncomfortable.

"She just," Dixie continues, "she hasn't ever been the same since I left."

"Left where?" I ask.

"The church, Ruby. The fucking Kingdom?"

She dramatically uses her index finger and points upward as if she is giving me directions to its exact geographical location.

"They don't make that decision easy on nobody. You pay to be there, but if truth be told, you pay far more to leave," she adds. "But enough of that! I am getting married in two days! Married, Ruby! Me! Married! Can you even imagine?"

WEEDS THROUGH THE FLOORBOARDS

I can't imagine. I attempt all efforts to be happy for Dixie. But deep within my sinful soul, I am dreadfully jealous.

I am jealous at the realization that this will never happen for me. I will never walk down an aisle on the arm of a daddy who gives away this woman to another woman. I will never wear a shimmering white dress with satin heels and my dead grandmother's pearls.

I will never have family sitting in the pews, wiping away tears of joy as they envy and feel compassion for the love I have found. I will never walk down an aisle to Annette or any other woman. The certainties of my uncertainties are forever trampled into my heart. I envy Dixie. I want to go to church with her and marry Annette.

Dixie interrupts my pretend wedding ceremony thoughts.

"Okay, girlfriend, today is a special day for us. We are gonna have some girlfriend time. I wanna take you to the church so you can help me decide what color of flowers I should get from the Piggly Wiggly floral department. I like the purple carnations with the yellow baby's breath, but I was thinking about how you got such a creative eye and all. I want your opinion. What do ya say?"

"Well, I would be honored," I respond, and that is truthful, something I am usually not.

"Oh, that is great! Bobby is meeting us there. We are gonna practice our I dos and—oh, wait! I almost forgot."

She stops abruptly and once again rummages through her purse. She proudly hands me a small blue box with a bright-green bow.

"Well, don't just sit there! Open it!"

I slowly open the box. I've never received an officially wrapped gift before. We don't give gifts in the Kingdom. The only gifts come from above, not from humans.

My fingers lift the delicate tissue paper, and there, beautifully placed on a small felt pedestal is a brilliant ruby. The stone shimmers in the afternoon sun, and its fiery color shadows one side of the box. It is shaped into a perfect circle. I gently pick it up and feel the smoothness, which reminds me of very little in my life right now. Nothing is smooth.

"It's so beautiful, Aunt Dixie! I love it! Thank you!"

"I just wanted you to have something special, something just for you."

There is no chain attached. Dixie understands, as I do, that there is no adornment of any sort when you are in the Kingdom. I appreciate her foresight. She knows the rules. She just doesn't obey them.

"Now I am workin' on your momma right now," Dixie interrupts as if she's walking around inside my head. "We still got a few hours to convince her that God will not smite the shit out of her if she actually comes to my wedding in a Catholic church."

She laughs at her own sense of humor.

Momma has not been silent about her disappointment with Dixie's choice to get married to Bobby Ray Montgomery, much less at the Holy Rosary. The entire Pine Creek Pentecostal congregation whispers their concerns and disappointments as well.

We drive in silence before slowly pulling into the church parking lot. Bobby is standing on the steps, looking up at the sky.

"What on earth? What is Bobby doing on the steps?" Dixie asks in confusion.

I immediately notice an alarming plume of thick black smoke billowing from the bell tower. Dixie slams the car in park and jumps out wildly as she runs to the steps.

"What the fuck!" she screams as she is officially in full sprint mode.

Can you scream *fuck* on the front steps of a church? Is that even allowed?

I leap out of the car and run after Dixie, who is wailing and flailing her arms as we both witness bright-red flames encompass the entire building. I hear sirens in the distance. I watch Dixie drop to her knees.

"What is happening right now!" she screams to no one.

I try to console her. Bobby kneels next to her on the ground as she pounds the pavement and lashes out at anyone near her, especially Bobby. I feel sorry for him.

All I can do is stand and observe as my left hand attempts to make its way to my hair. Instead, I reach deep inside my pocket and

WEEDS THROUGH THE FLOORBOARDS

find my ruby. I vigorously rub the soft stone over and over and over. Even in its smoothness, it does not grant me the release of my ceremonial twisting ritual.

My mind races, right along with my heart. I wonder how this could happen. I wonder if Dixie will recover. I wonder if Piggly Wiggly offers refunds. And I just can't help but wonder if Uncle Kevin is in town.

Chapter 13

FREEZER BURN

Momma does something I would never have expected in the entirety of my already established, short life. In the emotional aftermath of our situation, she asks me to stay with Dixie. I am actually honored that I am officially in charge of The Dixie, but I am not sure what to do for her.

She spends all day in bed, passed out, and drinks countless shots of whiskey and snorts train lines of cocaine all night through a sawed-in-half McDonald's straw. She does not eat—will not eat. I make countless attempts to give her food, to give her water, and she simply will not eat. She doesn't shower, and I hear her attempt to hide her pain-ridden sobs from her bedroom.

I am officially worried. While I am at school, I worry she will graciously perform a Betty Swan Dive routine; and when I am not at school, I worry that I will perform the Betty Swan Dive routine. Dixie has proven herself to be a full-time job for me.

Momma does not check on us. I don't mind it. For the very first time, I feel like an actual adult. Momma trusts me to take care of our private family crisis. I feel needed and necessary. But all that changes when Dixie decides to totally fuck up the already fucked up situation.

If the total truth be told, we all have to be good at something. I am good at keeping secrets. Momma is good at hiding them. Dixie is beyond exceptional at fucking things up. Royally.

It is Wednesday. I remember this because since I've been entrusted with Dixie's well-being, I've been exempt from Slideshow Wednesdays with the congregation. I arrive at the trailer park from school. Dixie's station wagon is parked near the front door. It really needs to be washed, like our sins.

I slip the key into the door, only for the door to slowly creep open. Dixie never leaves the door open. Never. You leave a door unlocked in the Lamplighter Trailer Park? Let's just say you will be robbed completely blind in broad daylight while you sip coffee at your kitchen table.

I cautiously step into the trailer, which is quiet and still.

"Dixie?" I shout.

No answer.

"Dixie? Are you here?" I call out again as I walk down the hall to the bedroom.

A feeling of dread rises up in my chest. Something feels wrong. I open her bedroom door, and there she is, sitting on the edge of the bed, rocking back and forth and staring blankly at the wall. Her face is puffy and red. There is nothing there—no light, no life, and no emotion. My heart breaks for my aunt.

"Oh, Dixie," I say lovingly as I press my body next to her on the bed and place my arms around her. "It's okay, Dixie. I've got you. Everything is okay. I am here. I love you, and I am here. I'm not gonna leave you. We will get through this. I promise."

She gently leans over and places her head trustingly on my shoulder.

We continue this therapeutic arrangement for several minutes in total silence until she sits up, laughs, and says, "Ya know what? Ruby Jane, I think I am finally ready to eat."

"Well, this is a start. That's real good, Dixie. I am going to make you the best meal you've ever had. You are gonna feel much better after we clean you up and get some food in you. We will paint our fingernails, eat popcorn, and watch *Wheel of Fortune*. Now how does that sound?"

Dixie loves *Wheel of Fortune*—R, S, T, L, N, E Vanna.

She softly smiles, and I see the smallest glimmer of light in her eyes, which I've not seen in a long while. I reach for her hands, take them in mine, and squeeze tightly. Her hands are ice-cold.

"I am just going to grab some food out of the fridge and whip us up a fabulous meal. You just wait. It is going to be just what you need," I promise.

Dixie stares firmly at me.

"No, no, no, Ruby, don't open the fridge," she says as she throws me her car keys. "Take the car and grab takeout from the Catfish Hole. I sure love that place. Make sure you order the hush puppies. I just love their hush puppies."

She lights a cigarette and blows the smoke out of the trailer window.

"Dixie," I say, "come on now. You know I don't have a license. And there is plenty of food in the fridge, and I really don't mind—"

She cuts me off, screaming, "There is also plenty of Bobby in the fridge!"

"What?" I shout. "What did you just say to me?"

I cannot breathe. I cannot breathe. I cannot breathe. I am looking for the exit row.

"What are you saying? Dixie, you are scaring me right now."

I gently place my hands on each side of her face and force her to look me in the eye.

"Dixie, look at me. What is going on? Why would you even think about saying something like that?"

"Bobby is in the fridge, Ruby. He's in the fridge, and I don't need you asking any fucking questions right now—or ever, for that fact. You will learn, questions ain't never good when you find yourself in certain unfortunate situations. You hear me, Ruby Jane? Look at me!"

I slowly raise my glance to meet hers.

"Yes, I hear you."

WEEDS THROUGH THE FLOORBOARDS

"Now how about those hush puppies?"

*****

I can't sleep. I contemplate choices and consequences legally and morally. I sit stone-faced in the kitchen and stare endlessly at the refrigerator all night and cannot collect the nerve to fucking open it. Dixie, however, is sleeping like a baby, something she hasn't done since the Unfortunate Pyromania Event at the Holy Rosary.

A small bald spot is slowly appearing where I have twisted and detached my hair from the scalp.

It is 5:00 a.m. Dixie Anne Thomas waltzes her ass into the kitchen in a Chinese silk robe and slippers that are encompassed in what looks like fake squirrel fur.

"Good morning, sunshine!" she cheerfully exclaims as I remain staring at the makeshift morgue.

"Seriously?" I reply. "At the risk of sounding like every member of our family, what the fuck is wrong with you?"

She turns her head quickly as if I have slapped her in the face.

"You just told me fucking Bobby is in your fridge, and you come up in here acting like we are going to fucking Disneyland? Is he really in there?" I ask, nodding my head toward the fridge.

"Yes, he is. I already told you to not ask questions, Ruby. Now I'm gonna need you to go to school and to keep your fucking mouth shut."

I am good at keeping secrets.

"Well, I am not going to school. I know that for sure! I am not going anywhere, for that matter. I am staying here with you."

I don't know what else to say. My words are just not there.

We sit quietly for a few minutes when I offer, "Is there anything I can do for you while we figure all this out?"

Without a moment's hesitation, Dixie Anne Thomas lights up and smiles.

"Well, since you asked, I could use some help cleaning out the fridge."

*****

We wait until no one can see us. I am used to not being seen. We wait and wait and wait. Secrets take time.

Dixie finally walks to the fridge and slowly opens the door, and there is Bobby. He is in a crouched position with gray duct tape around his eyes. There is a visible tiny circular red pinhole on his left temple. I immediately turn my head and vomit onto the linoleum floor.

"Don't be so fucking dramatic, Ruby," says Dixie. "He's fucking dead. Trust me, the only person missing this son of a bitch right now is his parole officer, and even that is questionable."

I breathe deep into my lungs. How could this have happened? How on earth did Bobby Ray Montgomery end up between the mustard and the baking soda? How are we going to get rid of a dead body that is in a fucking refrigerator in OUR kitchen? I am at a loss. This is not what I do best. This is not what I do at all. I fucking hate mustard.

Sensing my impending, complete nervous breakdown, Dixie gently places her hand on my hand. She brushes her fingers across my upper palm, a move that helps calm me.

"Ruby, please don't worry, baby girl. Everything is already taken care of. I need you to trust me. I need you to trust us."

There is a knock on the door at this exact moment. This type of knock is different. It feels permanent. Dixie opens the door and smiles. She is so beautiful when she smiles.

He confidently walks in and immediately embraces Aunt Dixie. They hold each other in the doorway.

"It's so good to see you, Dixie Anne."

His voice is deep and sounds safe. He glances at me and shifts his affections.

"Well, look at you, Ruby Jane, all grown up. If you aren't the spitting image of your momma! If I didn't know better, I would think you were Susie Q herself."

"Hi, Uncle Kevin," I respond.

Oh, sweet mother of baby Jesus.

"So"—he sets his suitcase down and claps and brushes his hands together—"I hear we have another hole to dig."

*****

I breathe the cigarette smoke deep into my body, praying the harsh toxins will rot away memories. I literally Pentecostal-pray down on my knees that the last twenty-four hours of my life will fade away just like the headlights of Dixie's car as she and Uncle Kevin disappear into the middle of the night.

I feel something like nothingness. My heart is numb. For a brief moment, I think of Grandma and her Jesus Saves Garden. I can't help but hope that wherever Bobby Ray Montgomery ends up tonight, he will be in a really nice garden…facing east.

Chapter 14

KUNG FU PRINCESS

It has been four months, one week, and three days since the Unfortunate Bobby-With-A-Side-Of-Mustard Debacle. Not one word has been spoken. Not one question has been asked. Life moves on for all of us—except Bobby, of course.

When I hear sirens in the distance, my pulse races; my heart beats; and in my head, I visualize the police skidding into the parking lot of the school, throwing me up against the squad car, and binding my wrists with handcuffs. But that never happens.

My birthday is in three days. I am not sure why I celebrate the day of my being brought into this world. I don't belong here. I don't fit in. I cannot be me. I find it far more understandable that I celebrate the day I will leave.

However, for my birthday, Netti arranges for us to stay the night at her cousin Rayna's house under the strict parental premise that we are house-sitting while Rayna goes to Little Rock to do God's work. This makes all the parents happy. Netti and I have never spent the entire night together by ourselves like adults.

It is a Saturday. Our parents have graciously allowed us to help our sister in Christ with the full expectation that we will be prompt for Sunday service and worship. We spend our evening lying in the backyard, staring up at the stars.

She points up at the sky.

"You see that big one? I'm naming that after you, Ruby Jane."

I laugh.

"You can't name stars after people, Netti!"

"And why the hell not?" she continues. "I can do anything I want. I like that star. It's how my insides feel when I'm with you."

She squeezes my hand.

There are moments when I have an impulse to blurt out, "Bobby Ray was in the fridge, and Uncle Kevin buried him in the Jesus Saves Garden!" But I always stop myself. I don't want to put that secret on anyone else but me. It's one thing to have secrets. But secrets like that come with tremendous responsibility.

Netti jumps up and brushes off her knees.

"I have a surprise for you!"

In my head, I am thinking, *You don't know the word* surprise *until you open the fridge for mustard.*

"Wait two minutes, and then come inside."

And then she is gone. I impatiently wait, counting seconds in my head. I slide the patio door open and step inside. I can see the hallway dimly lit and the bedroom door open. When I walk into the bedroom, candles engulf the room. Their tiny, flickering tips feel like the flames themselves are celebrating what is going to happen next.

There is a glass of sweet pink muscadine wine on the nightstand next to the bed. Annette is seated on the bed, wearing nothing more than herself. She takes my hand gently, pulls me into the sheets, and straddles me. The orange glow of the flames forms a distinctive, comforting shade around her face. She is so fucking beautiful.

She kisses me. This time, it's different. Her tongue feels heavy and full, demanding. I feel a stir between my legs like I've never felt in my life. She starts at the very tip of my head, kissing and brushing her tongue tenderly as she works her way down my entire body.

She stops at my nipple and begins a circular motion that gets faster and faster. I can no longer hold in my desire. I pant and take a deep breath in. She continues to trace my entire body with her tongue as she works her way between my legs.

She enters me with her tongue and playfully darts in and out until I am literally begging. I come so hard that my entire body shakes. But as in the Ronco commercials, "But wait. There's more!" I come again and again and again and again, each orgasm more intense than the first.

When I think I cannot come anymore, she looks up at me from between my legs and softly says, "I decide when you are done."

Afterward, I lay in complete stillness. She curls up next to me, places her arms around me, and rubs her fingers over my bald patch, on the top-left corner of my scalp.

"I love you, Ruby Jane."

It's at this exact moment that I realize for the very first time in my life, God doesn't love me as much as Netti does. He actually hates me. He hates everything I am, and he hates more of what I am not. He hates who I love and even more who I cannot love. He hates me for all the secrets I keep and for all the commandments I don't.

It's official. The wheels have come off my trailer.

*****

"Lesbo. Homo."
"Kitty licker. Cunt sticker."
"Wish a dick. Found a clit."
"Undercover black man lover."
"Beaver eater. Pussy fever."
"Nipple sucker. Queer fucker."
"Rah, rah, rah."

My daily walks through the high school hallways provide me with the pleasure of these unremarkable remarks. Clearly, these are brazen attempts to place me into the category "We don't take too kindly to you folks in these parts."

WEEDS THROUGH THE FLOORBOARDS

Netti isn't subjected to these rants, because she has been home-schooled since sixth grade. This is actually a good thing. Talking to my Netti that way will only open a can of whoop-ass from none other than the most famous lesbian in Yell County.

Unfortunately for the most famous lesbian in Yell County, that can of whoop-ass is opened like a Mountain Dew shaken vigorously for far too long. And on this day, Gaby Newton pops the top.

I am waiting at the bus stop. It is a Thursday.

"Well, would you look at this! A real live Jesus-freak girl fucker right here!" she jeers, making efforts to draw a crowd around us.

Her efforts are successful. Others swarm around and form a chain-link slinky around the two of us.

"Well, say something, you stupid bitch."

She takes both of her hands and shoves them into my chest so violently it takes me by surprise, and I fall flat onto the ground. This prompts a roar of laughter from the curious asshole onlookers, who act like they are front row for NASCAR.

"You are so pathetic," Gaby says, continuing her rant as she kicks dirt into my face.

She places her left Converse on my right hand, slowly crushing it against the hard ground. I take a deep breath in as I calmly search for the exit row. Something overwhelms me, and this time, it feels different from before. I am no longer looking left to right, around and down, to locate an exit strategy. I visualize a sign above my head that reads Enter With Caution. Fuck caution.

I spring to my feet, pull my right arm back as far as humanly possible, and punch Gaby Newton right in the face. This isn't what I consider to be a normal fight punch. This is more of a punch that could quite possibly end this bitch up in the Bobby-With-A-Side-Of-Mustard Fridge.

I hear bones in my hand crushing, and blood is squirting every-where. It takes a moment for me to comprehend the blood is not coming from me. It is coming from Gaby's head, her mouth, and her nose.

Gaby violently screams while holding both of her hands to her face. She is crying at the top of her lungs, and her words are incomprehensible. Yes, I've made my point successfully. Yes, everyone looks scared shitless right now. Yes, I could stop here, and problem solved. But no, I am not done.

I tackle her like a professional athlete and pin her entire body to the ground as I punch her in every bodily place that is available. She attempts to protect her head with her hands. In return, I grab both of her hands and hold them useless under the weight of my legs.

I then use my own head as a fierce weapon. I headbutt her over and over and over—one headbutt for every secret. I am bleeding profusely, and damn, it feels good.

Eventually, I am physically lifted into the air by strong arms that pull me away while I continue to air-punch, throat-punch, and fuck-you-punch anything in my reach. I stand up to see a mass of students who have gathered, gawking at me, most with their mouths open, unable to speak.

Gaby, on the other hand, is dramatically sobbing uncontrollably, holding her nose and screaming at the top of her lungs that she's gonna tell her momma, which makes everyone laugh at her.

Composing myself, I spit a long string of blood from my mouth and make an attempt to shift my nose back into place. I wipe the open gash on my head with the sleeve of my shirt. My eyes burn as flowing streams of blood coat them and trickle to the ground.

I turn to leave, stopping only to present myself to the crowd and boldly announce, "If any of you ever talk to me like that again, as God is my fucking witness, I will personally slit your throat from ear to ear, then slit it again, cut you into tiny pieces, and feed you to old man Miller's hogs. If you don't believe that, I am willing to take on the next fucker in line. Come on! Let's do this!"

I wait. There is nothing but scared, fucking pathetic faces staring back, looking at one another as if trying to escape my wrath.

"That's a good call 'cause the next one of you that comes at me? I will kill you. Rest assured."

I heroically walk away, my strut confident. I lean my head back, and a wave of hysterical laughter pours from my throat. I don't know where it is coming from. I can't control it. I bend my entire body over

WEEDS THROUGH THE FLOORBOARDS

to try and catch my breath as the blood spills from my wounds to the grass as the crowd stares at me in utter horror.

I glance down to see a small group of withered green weeds with beige buds and tiny white stems. The patterns of the splattered blood decorate them as if dressing them in a different wardrobe, like soldiers fighting to stay alive. I understand. The weeds are dressed in blood. I am just dressed in secrets.

*****

I am officially suspended for two weeks. I also officially don't care. This is actually favorable timing for me. I need this time to recover. My body is utterly racked with pain, and my head offers brutally open wounds thanks to the ratio of headbutts to secrets.

I am in desperate need of medical bandages. I need stitches. I need ice. I need aspirin. And according to Momma, I really need Jesus.

Momma and Daddy don't say much. The house remains eerily quiet of conversations and accusations. There are no questions asked, which means no answers are required. Like everything in my life, they would rather not know.

It is day four of my nonmedical infirmary commitment. There is no doubt that I need to see a doctor. There is also no doubt that I will not be able to see a doctor. God is the only physician. We don't do doctors. We don't do medicine. We rely only and solely on faith-based healing—Dirt Tea.

This is confusing to someone like me. How do you have faith healing when you have no faith? I have no hope. I have no God. I am empty. And although Momma and Daddy call upon the entire congregation to pray over me, to activate their faith-healing rituals, and to raise their hands to the heavens and shout out in unrecognizable tongues, my wounds stay open, my heart stays closed, and nothing heals. Nothing ever heals.

Three days later, we find Daddy dead in the driveway, slumped over the steering wheel of his white Ford pickup truck. It is all my fault. They've used up all their faith-healing prayers on me.

Chapter 15

ASK AND YE SHALL RECEIVE

After Daddy makes his exit strategy to the Kingdom, I meticulously plan my days and my nights, smoking enormous amounts of weed, snorting enough cocaine to put the cartel on full alert, swallowing rainbows of pills with unknown consequences, and fucking Netti in ways that could land me into the Porn Star Academy Hall of Fame.

What I admire about drugs is that they are incredibly genteel and polite.

"It's such a pleasure to meet you."

"Would you just look at your beautiful smile."

"You feel absolutely amazing, Ruby Jane."

"It is so nice to see you again."

"If there is anything you need, please just let me know."

"I will never ever leave you. I will always be here whenever you call."

Drugs are devoted to you more than anything else on this earth. Drugs don't judge. They embrace you endlessly and effortlessly.

Drugs adore and capture your inability to feel. They appreciate your capacity to ignore your emotions. Drugs enjoy your complete lack of respect. Simply put, they are a good friend when you need one. Drugs listen.

I now spend more and more time with Aunt Dixie. Momma is inherently nonexistent—to me or to anyone. I don't take it personally. If God's truth be told, I attempt every effort to accommodate this unfortunate situation emotionally. I understand Daddy is settled for the Rapture, but I am still here. I am not seen.

To be honest, I prefer to be with Dixie. We are two peas in a pod, or rather, two peas in a trailer. I do whatever I want. I eat whenever I want. I go to school whenever I want. I sleep in whenever I want. I fuck Netti whenever I want. I skip church whenever I want.

Dixie makes me feel like I will actually be someone someday. She talks to me for hours and understands everything I need. We share our feelings and our hopes, our drugs and our secrets. Dixie is my biggest cheerleader, something I've never known. No one has ever cheered for me. Team Ruby!

One Saturday night, while Netti is visiting for our daily Slip-and-Slide Session, Dixie jumps straight up from her chair; grabs her jacket, her purse, and a six-pack of beer; and commands us in her cheerleading voice, "You know what we all could use right now? We need some fun, some excitement in our lives!"

This comment makes me terribly anxious considering in the past, Dixie plus excitement typically equates to a night in the slammer or a duct-taped body in a freezer.

"Come on!" she yells while motioning for us to follow her.

We all pile in like soldiers following direct orders from Commander Dixie.

"Where are we headed?" I ask as we settle into the car.

"Oh, sweetie, we are going to take a quick road trip. I have a big surprise for the two of you. Now sit back, pop a beer for us, and enjoy the ride."

We drive for an hour—windows down, radio up, beer flowing, and weed blowing. Our impromptu journey ends as we slowly pull into a parking lot off Interstate 40. Dixie stops the car, tousles her hair, and looks to the rearview mirror for a beauty check before exiting the car.

"This is going to be so much fun!" she adds, walking toward an enormous warehouse surrounded by shining, bright light bulbs and a beautiful sign blinking the word Discovery.

There is an extended line of people wrapped completely around the building. There are more people here than at the annual Pine Creek Pentecostal Revival, and that is saying a lot considering the revival covers the entire tristate area.

"Come on, girls. It's time for some well-deserved fuckupedness."

"Dixie? We cannot do this. We are not old enough to go in there. You know that. It's a, ya know, a bar," I remind her.

"Oh, for fuck's sake, Ruby Jane. Are you always so fucking negative? You literally sound like a goddamn Sunday school teacher right now, and you actually are dressed close to one. No offense, but we gotta work on your game.

"Do you think your Aunt Dixie doesn't have this shit handled? Not to brag, but I've fucked about every bouncer and bartender in this place. Oh, and stay away from Calvin. His dick is the size of the Mississippi River. That thing will bust your throat wide open."

Dixie prances straight up to the front of the line and flirtatiously leans up to whisper into the ear of an enormous man dressed in total black.

He smiles, opens the door, and warmly says, "Welcome, ladies," while using his arm to usher us through the walkway.

She has clearly committed to fucking him later, but who am I to judge?

When we walk through the door, the music immediately surrounds us. You can feel the base thumping inside of your chest. The bar is packed with random bodies, all seemingly having the time of their life. We carelessly float from room to room to room before settling in the very back, where my eyes are finally adjusting to the darkness.

Dixie leaves for the bar. Netti and I make ourselves comfortable on an old leather couch, not sure of what to do next. I try to keep the

WEEDS THROUGH THE FLOORBOARDS

appearance of someone who belongs here. But in my defense, this is my first bar. I am a Bar Virgin.

It is quickly becoming clear through the fog of smoke as I look around that there are countless women together—women of all ages, women of all colors, women dressed in jeans and flannel, women dressed in leather and heels, men dressed as women, women dressed as men, and women dancing, laughing, touching, kissing, and loving one another.

Dixie returns with three tiny glasses filled with a rainbow of colors.

"Open wide, bitches," she says as she graciously pops tiny blue pills on our tongues.

"Drink up, clit lickers!" she roars hysterically as we collectively chime our shot glasses together and chase our tiny blue pills down our throats. "Welcome to heaven," she adds as she disappears into the darkness.

Netti and I sink down into the couch and revel in our surroundings—the music, the rhythm, the lights, and the smell of sweat and sex. We begin to touch each other tenderly. It's one thing to love someone. It's another thing to love someone in front of others.

We hold each other effortlessly. We kiss wildly and passionately. Her hair smells like lilacs and cloves. I sink my nose into the crevice of her neck. I love the way she smells.

The tiny blue thingy, unbeknownst to me, kicks into full gear. My entire body feels like floating, weightless feathers, and Netti's touches feel like the glue holding us all together.

"Let's dance!" Netti shouts over the blaring music.

I am realizing I've never danced before. You don't dance when you are a member of the Kingdom.

"I don't know how!" I shout into her ear as we both giggle hysterically and race each other to the dance floor.

Suddenly, all the years of sinner altar calls, of Slideshow Wednesdays, of fire and brimstone, of suffocating sermons of hate and nonacceptance, of total fear, of Betty Swan Dives, of Granddaddy Tuesdays, and of Refrigerator Bobby have been released throughout all of my being; and I go insanely wild. My entire body is screaming and letting go, but only in movement.

Finally, I am seen. I am loving who I love in front of others. No one is judging. They are doing the same. I am free. We are free.

Freedom, however, like happiness, is short-lived.

Suddenly, my dazzling moment of finally being seen is expeditiously interrupted by a commotion of epic proportions. I glance toward the clamor just in time to witness Dixie physically throwing a woman over the pool table and crushing the pool stick over her head.

"You fucking cunt! You cheater!" she screams into her face.

I sprint to the scene in an honest effort to avoid a potential arrest. By the time I reach her, she is pounding the unknown victim with fists, legs, feet, and whatever will cause pain.

"You fucking liar! Give me my fucking money! I swear to God, I will put you in the goddamn fridge and bury your ass just like..."

I hurriedly shove my hand over her mouth. She is spewing the muffled words through my fingers. Although I am aware of the exact words she is screaming through my hands, it is most essential that others are not.

Dixie bites down hard into my skin, which triggers me to abruptly place her in a choke hold and pull her through the bar like a true *Jerry Springer* episode. Netti and I then attempt to drag Dixie by any and all means necessary through the parking lot. I say attempt because that is exactly what it is—an attempt. She is wild, batshit banshee crazy, clawing, pulling, and tearing at anything within her grasp, and that grasp includes me.

"Where is my money!" she continues to scream as we make our way to the car.

I am wiping blood from my nose and my hands as I literally slam her to the pavement and hold her body to the ground.

Netti feverishly digs through Dixie's purse with an urgent effort to locate the car keys. This leads to an unfortunate game of Hide-and-Seek. Not only do we locate the keys, we locate numerous bags of white powder pouring out onto the asphalt, a plethora of pills in all colors, bags bulging with weed, and one petite pink pistol lying effortlessly at the very bottom of the purse, which is more than likely

WEEDS THROUGH THE FLOORBOARDS

the tiny, petite weapon that assisted in Bobby Ray's most untimely demise.

We struggle with everything in us and finally manage to shove Dixie into the back seat. I grab the keys, the coke, the pills, the weed, and the purse; start the car; and literally flee the scene as two police cars roar into the parking lot with red-and-blue lights blaring and sirens screeching.

We are finally on the freeway, heading home. There is total silence. Each of us is reflecting on what just happened and what almost happened and most grateful for what didn't happen.

The silence is only broken when Dixie yells, "Y'all didn't have to be so fucking dramatic back there. I am fully capable of walking to a car unassisted, thank you very much."

"Oh, really?" I answer. "So just to be clear, instead of just leaving, you decide to possibly get all of us arrested because some bitch didn't pay you for a bag of coke? Seriously, Dixie? And we are the ones being dramatic?"

"What?" she replies in a completely astonished confusion.

This remark ensues into an uproar of outrageous laughter. Dixie lays down in the back seat, holding her chest and attempting to catch her breath.

"Are you fucking kidding me right now, Ruby Jane?" she shouts through her laughter. "You think I kicked her ass because she didn't pay me for some stupid fucking cocaine? You really are the most ignorant hillbilly I know. No offense. I know your momma, so I can't really blame you for it.

"I didn't kick her ass for not paying me for coke, Ruby. I kicked her ass because she owes me money for taking care of her worthless, piece-of-shit brother."

"What are you talking about?" I ask. "What brother?"

"You met him, for Christ's sake," she concludes. "In the fridge, next to the mustard."

*****

The next morning brings with it the distant sound of a weed eater, the irritating chirps of melodic birds, and the tumultuous body tremors of a hangover that will forever go down in history as The One.

I wake up half dressed and half high and lying on top of a pile of clothes on Dixie's bed. My head feels like I have the unfortunate Bobby Montgomery pinhole through the temple. I hear faint voices coming from the kitchen and the clanking of dishes, and I smell the welcoming fragrance of coffee and cigarettes.

I walk into the kitchen to see Dixie and Netti seated at the table, surrounded by remnants of last night's Hide-and-Seek adventure through Dixie's purse. A variety of pills is scattered across the tabletop. Visible lines of coke appear to have stopped mid sniff as if someone has decided that might be a bad decision. Rolling papers separate weed from seeds, and empty beer cans are methodically lined from left to right.

"Well, would you lookie here," Dixie says when I enter the kitchen. "Lesbian Sleeping Beauty has decided to grace us heathens with her presence. Oh, honey child, you seriously look like a big pile of hot dog shit. Here, baby girl," she says as she hands me two small white tablets from the Official Pill Library.

I don't hesitate. I pop them into my mouth, grab the open beer from Netti's hand, and swallow. The soft, warm foam coats my throat and calms my insides. It feels protective.

"Coffee's brewing. Coffee makes everything better."

Dixie smiles. She is so beautiful when she smiles.

"What time did y'all get up? It's eight in the morning, for God's sake. Does anyone ever sleep around here?" I ask.

"Get up?" Dixie responds. "Why, darling, we haven't gone to bed, you silly thing. If you learn anything from your Aunt Dixie, let it be this. You can't never have a hangover if you never go to bed."

On some level, this actually makes sense.

I pour my coffee, light a cigarette, and finish the unfinished line of coke on the table. I will gladly complete someone's bad decision.

There is a knock on the door. It is sudden. It feels invasive and makes me uneasy.

WEEDS THROUGH THE FLOORBOARDS

Dixie leaps out of her chair, peeps through the curtains above the kitchen sink, and silently screams, "It's your mother!"

The three of us scatter in three directions with Dixie's arm sweeping the contents of the table in one full swoop into a large blanket on the floor. Her skills are quite impressive, to say the least. Netti sprays Lysol like she is the tuberculosis police, and I make a pathetic attempt at arranging the living room in honor of Carol Brady.

All the while, Momma's knocking is becoming louder and more pronounced. Her insistence is unnerving. We all three signal to one another before Dixie opens the door cautiously.

"Well, good morning, Susie. It's good to see you. Come in. Come right on in," she greets, graciously inviting Momma inside. "Would you like some coffee?"

Momma reluctantly enters the trailer. This is a first. She appears suspicious as she attempts to assess the situation. Her eyes land directly on me.

"No coffee for me, Dixie. Thank you anyways. I just came to see Ruby," she answers coldly.

"Hi, Momma."

I have missed her.

"Hi, Ruby. I haven't heard from you in so long, so I just, well, I guess I just wanted to make sure you were doing okay. Pastor Eddie is asking for you. Oh, and for Netti. Hi, Netti," Momma adds as she glances in her direction. "It has been a while since you've been in church."

She clears her throat as if she is unsure of what to say.

"People are talking, Ruby. They say you've been drinking and smoking and staying out all hours of the night. They even say you like girls. Girls, Ruby. Do you, Ruby? Do you like girls in that kinda way? Because if this is true, I am beyond grateful to our Father God in heaven that your daddy is dead, because that would have killed him for sure.

"Look at you right now, Ruby, wearing pants, for God's sake in heaven. Our Lord and Savior is so broken for you right now. And is that mascara on your face?"

85

Momma continues relentlessly with her checklist of Items That Secure Your Entrance to Hell. I am mentally checking all the boxes.

"I wasn't even sure you would be here, Ruby. I got in my car this morning and prayed for God to lead me to you, and here I am. The congregation is asking for you to come to service on Wednesday, Ruby. Come home to us. There is forgiveness there. It is not my place to ask for Netti. But for you, Ruby? If you will come and ask for forgiveness, you will be welcomed back into the Kingdom. All you have to do is ask."

And then she waits. She waits for me to respond.

Hmm, all I have to do is ask. I look around the room and cannot help but sniff—not a crying, sad, emotional sniff but more of a "I just snorted a badass line of coke at my last Coke-Tail Happy Hour" sniff.

"I'm not coming back, Momma, not today, not ever. I don't fit in there," I finally respond as gently as possible.

I have no intention of returning, but I have every intention of not hurting Momma.

"But, Ruby, you are gonna end up in hell. I know you think you are grown, and you can make your own decisions. But I cannot be happy for you if this is your decision. I will never be happy for you."

This sounds like goodbye.

"Don't worry, Momma," I say, trying to comfort her. "Don't you spend another minute worrying yourself over any of this. I am not going to hell, Momma. I am already here."

Chapter 16

SCRAPS

"We need to talk," I say to Dixie that evening. "Now."

"Them are fighting words in this family. And for the love of God, what is it now? I swear, Ruby Jane, I really don't mean to hurt your feelings. But has anyone ever told you that quite frankly, you fucking talk too much?"

She casually crushes her half-smoked cigarette onto the top of an empty beer can and flips it inside the can with her finger. The smoke still simmers from the top as she shakes the leftover suds to deaden the ash.

"I need you to tell me what happened at the bar last night, Dixie. What is really going on? Hell, Netti keeps firing questions at me, asking what you were going on and on about in the car about a man and a fridge and mustard. I told her you have completely lost your mind inside all these drugs and that I have no idea what you were saying. It's dangerous to talk about these things in front of her. You cannot ever let this happen again," I plead.

Dixie slowly releases a deliberate, extended sigh as if she is releasing tucked-away memories that have crushed her chest and are now lifting the weight to allow her to breathe just for a moment. Secrets can suffocate.

"Bobby is—I mean, how do I put this?" she asks her own self with a true tone of reflection. "Bobby is—I mean, Bobby was—not worthy of the ground I spit on," she concludes.

"Dixie, wait a minute, wait a minute. You cannot just say things like that. You were gonna marry him, Dixie. Why would you want to marry someone and then say such a horrible thing about them?" I ask, waiting for the answer.

"Bobby? I am about to tell you the truth, but you can never ever speak of this again. You hear me?"

I nod my head in agreement but also feel the burden and wrath of another secret set to be graciously bestowed upon me.

"Bobby was, well, quite frankly, he was nothing more than a worn-out piece of shit, Ruby Jane. He never did nothing for me but beat me and use me for my drugs. He was a mean man, Ruby. You have no idea the things he did, things I allowed him to do. Trust me, there was a reason."

I have never heard Dixie express this tone before. She speaks as if broken and far away in the distance, like she is speaking to someone not really here or there or anywhere, for that matter. She stares blankly straight ahead and continues.

"He did something awful to his sister, Norma Mae. She was the one at the bar," she confesses. "We went to school together, all of us—me and your momma and Norma. She was a good friend to your momma and me. She helped us anytime we asked. And, baby girl, we needed a lot of help. There are some things you just don't know and don't need to know. Our life was not a good one, Ruby. It was just, well, really difficult."

Her voice softens as she remembers.

"Sometimes, things happened that are so awful, I don't even want to speak it into the universe, because speaking them into the universe brings nothing but sorrow."

She is almost whispering now to make sure no one hears, although we are the only two people in the room.

"Our momma—well, your grandmother—she wasn't the most stable person, ya know what I'm sayin'? Our momma? She was cruel. She was so cruel, and she…well, she did things that your momma and me will never speak of, not ever."

I confidently nod my head. I am not the most stable person either. I would benefit immensely from a warning sign furiously blinking around my neck, reading, "Unstable. Do not touch."

"There were some times, Ruby Jane, when our momma would leave. She would just completely disappear, sometimes for months at a time. Your momma and me and Uncle Kevin? We were just kids. We had no food, no way of getting food, no electricity. We had nothing.

"The worst part is that we never knew how long she was gonna be gone. We was scared all the time. But we took care of each other. Or at least we tried. And when she would return? She was abusive and crazy as a loon.

"We wasn't ever sure of where those long absences took her to, but we were sure that wherever it was, she took it out on all of us when she would come home. And your Uncle Kevin? He got the brunt of it. She was something awful to him."

Dixie's voice cracks, and a small tear pushes from her eye. She rapidly brushes her palms under her eyes as if to erase any witness of her caring.

I remain as still as possible. I don't want to interrupt this confession of truth. It is evident as Dixie speaks that these words have never come out before, and my heart hurts for her. I can see pain in her eyes like she is still a small, innocent child waiting for Grandma to come home.

"Well, it was during this time that Norma's family always took us in. They would feed us and make sure we had clean clothes. And Norma's momma, Ms. Linda? Why, she was nothing short of an angel on earth.

"Ms. Linda didn't love us or nothin' like that. She had pity for us. She would look at us like we was stray dogs that needed scraps. But let me tell you something, Ruby Jane. Those scraps saved us. It was the only sort of love that we ever felt."

She looks to me with compassion and such sorrow that I feel it too.

"What about Grandpa? Where was he? Why didn't he help?" I ask.

Dixie becomes noticeably uncomfortable and shifts her weight around, adjusts her skirt, and makes it clear that I have severed a nerve.

"Well, Ruby, honey, I'm just not gonna talk about that, except to say, well, to say that your grandpa never really took a likin' to being a father. When our momma would leave for months on end, he used that time to escape us as well. No one wanted us. No one."

"But you were gonna marry Bobby. I don't understand. What? What did he do? Dixie, tell me. I need to understand what happened to him. It's not like Bobby moved out of town, or he went away, or y'all broke up. Dixie, he is dead, and I saw him. I deserve to know."

"He…"

She pauses.

"He got her pregnant, Ruby."

"He got Momma pregnant?"

"Oh no, not your momma, Ruby. Norma. He got Norma pregnant."

Dixie rushes to place her hand over her mouth as if shocked the words have escaped.

"His own sister, Ruby. His own blood. I mean, what kind of a monster does that make him? True enough, it was years ago. But still, he did it."

She fades away. I sit in shock. I think it is shock.

"What? How do you know this? Who told you this? Dixie, you know you have my confidence, and I haven't breathed a fucking word of anything. But this? This is an unforgivable thing to say if it's not true," I respond.

"Oh, it's true, all right. I know it's true because I was there. I mean, I wasn't *there*, there. But I—or we, your momma and me— took her to get an abortion."

She closes her eyes as if reliving the memory.

"We were only a few years older than you are now, Ruby."

I am listening, and although I am trying to find the words to respond, I am still hook, line, and sinker on the Momma Abortion Committee Confession.

"We've spent all these years deciding how to make him pay for such an unspeakable act. Our plan just, well, just didn't go as planned," she says.

"What do you mean? What did you plan?"

I am now overwhelmed by what I've just learned.

"Oh, honey, there's no need to bother yourself with all these ancient details. As we say in Yell County, it's water under the bridge. I like to call it whiskey under the bridge, but it is what it is. Now you know. You know the truth. Yes, we had plans. Those plans didn't go as planned. So our new plans just happened to include a refrigerator and a shovel. The end."

"But the church...I saw you at the church. I was there. We were picking colors for the Piggly Wiggly order for flowers, and you...you were crying and sobbing, and...I still don't..."

She interrupts me with a fit of crazy laughter.

"Oh, Ruby, honey, you poor, innocent creature you. Honey, I wasn't crying because the church was burning. I was crying because that son of a bitch was supposed to be burning in it."

She is now bent over, cackling uncontrollably and crying at the same time—crying in a comedic way, not a sorrowful way. I sit in complete silence. I cannot believe this is happening. The little air that I feel is heavy in my lungs, and without notice, a tear makes its way from my eye and down to my chin.

"Someone needs to take your matches away, Aunt Dixie," I add in an attempt to lighten the mood.

Without hesitation, Dixie says, "My matches? You are so funny, baby girl—funny but a bit fucking stupid. You better check your momma's purse before you come digging through mine."

Chapter 17

LICKETY-SPLIT

I am just days away from summer vacation, and I could not be happier. I despise school. I have no friends, and no one likes me. I am completely alone—alone at lunch, alone in class, and alone in life.

Since Momma kicked me out of the Kingdom, I have occupied the couch at Dixie's. I do, however, have an impressive full-time job rating all her drugs on a scale from one to I can't feel my face. It's not a bad gig.

Dixie and I spend our nights relaxing on the front porch of the trailer, poking fun at all the residents who live on welfare, Marlboro Lights, and wheels.

We all know Cindy Palmer's last baby ain't Mr. Palmer's on account of his skin having a tint of milk chocolate. Mr. Palmer doesn't seem to mind, probably because he has four other kids to choose from if need be.

Mr. Harris, who lives in the very last trailer on the lot, manufactures bathtub crank and fucks everyone but Mrs. Harris. We all just

Hail Mary and pray Mr. Harris doesn't blow the entire park up with his meth antics. So far, so good.

Lacy Dobbs is the village idiot, bless her heart. She means well, but we all know she is slower than sap and will probably never be on the receiving end of a good fuck.

It is Friday, the last day before summer break begins. This day will change my life forever. I head to Dixie's after my last day of school, carrying not only my unopened textbooks but also the highest hopes of celebrating summer freedom. It's not like Dixie and I don't celebrate something every single day already. It's more like a celebration of my being free for an entire ten weeks. I have big plans for us.

I've always wanted to learn how to swim—not just wade into water and splash around on account of the water being bathtub deep but really swim—because in so many moments in my life, I feel I'm drowning.

I've never been allowed to swim, because that would require one to wear a bathing suit. And when you are a member of the Kingdom, bathing suits are not only prohibited but are also shameful and can be the direct cause of lustful and desirous thoughts and actions.

As kids, we were not even allowed to play in the river behind the church during Bible school. It was 102 degrees in the middle of summer, but soaking our feet in the river was biblically restricted on account of us having to show leg skin by raising our skirts.

This never sat well with me. Wasn't Jesus baptized in the Jordan River? When I asked Daddy one time why Jesus could be baptized in the river and we couldn't, he explained that was why the church had a baptismal tank. We could crawl in, be submerged, and crawl out, all without anyone seeing our wet clothes clinging to our bodies. It sounded like the local Grab and Go—a one-stop shop.

As I finally arrive at Dixie's trailer, I use my key to open the door. I step inside, half expecting Dixie to be cheering and rooting me on in the living room, offering the rainbow of sheer happiness; that rainbow being Xanax, Trazodone, Methadone, uppers, downers, smilers, and frowners.

It is no secret that I no longer enter Dixie's trailer without first and foremost assessing the contents of the refrigerator. You just never know.

But Dixie is nowhere in sight.

"Hello?" I call.

There is no answer.

"Hello, Dixie? Are you here?"

And then I hear muffled voices from the bedroom. I walk down the hall and cautiously lean my ear against the door, making certain to not disturb her privacy, knowing full well that she could have god knows who handcuffed to her bedposts while holding them ransom for money. This thought makes me giggle out loud.

I crack the door ever so slightly. As I lean in, my heart dramatically drops to my feet, and my head spirals into what I know will happen next. I completely open the bedroom door, and there it is—Dixie lying on her back, legs spread wide open, thrusting her bony hips into the tongue of none other than Annette, my Annette, my Netti.

My entire body begins to shake. I cover my mouth in an attempt to muffle out the scream that escapes. I turn and run as fast as I can. I hear Dixie shouting to me, but I do not stop. I run and run and run and run. I don't know what to do. What I do know for sure is that someone needs to take away my Swan Dive and Lifetime movie packing scarves and red leggings...just in case.

*****

It is 6:43 a.m. I slowly wake up in my own bed, comforted by nothing other than the familiarity of my own blankets and the softness of a pillow that embraces my head, my heart, my sadness, and my secrets. I am home.

Momma has not spoken to me since my marathon run home. Momma asks no questions. Momma says nothing. We appreciate the silence of secrets.

It is day four of my reenactment of the Prodigal Son Returns Tour when Momma finds it within herself to form human words and inquire as to why I am there.

WEEDS THROUGH THE FLOORBOARDS

"Ruby Jane, I don't know what happened. I am not even sure that I wanna know. But Dixie has been calling here nonstop, asking for you. What is going on? Did something happen? You can talk to me. Did you all have a fuss?" she asks innocently.

"A fuss? Is that what you think, Momma? A fuss? Is that what she told you, Momma?"

I am so exhausted. I am bitter and well beyond broken. I am defeated from fighting. I need someone to fight for me.

"A fuss? No, Momma, we did not have a stupid fuss. A fuss would be not picking up my clothes on the floor or not putting gas in the car. A fuss would be not turning off the lights when you leave. No, we didn't have a fuss! She is fucking my girlfriend!" I scream.

"She was the only person in my life that made me feel loved, Momma, the only one—not you, not Daddy, not anyone. Do you know what that is like? Netti was my entire life, and the only other person in this world that I thought loved me decided to spread her fucking legs and let my girlfriend fuck her! No, I am NOT okay!" I finish.

I am completely weakened from my unexpected reaction.

"You better stop right there, Ruby Jane. You know better! I didn't raise you this way. You will not talk to me that way. I will not allow you to use those sinful words in front of God and our—"

"God and fucking who?" I interrupt. "God and—oh, maybe God and Norma?"

Momma's face freezes in place, and her eyes dart directly to me. She is afraid, and I can see it.

"Maybe God and Bobby?" I continue. "I would ask God about Bobby, but you and I both know he is face down in his own Garden of Eden, paying for what he did to Norma."

Momma is physically shaking, and I can visually see her mind racing as to what Dixie has done and what Dixie has shared with me. This is where secrets lead, right here where we stand. But wait. There's more.

"Or perhaps we can reach out to God and inquire about the proposed Bobby bonfire?"

Momma seethes and looks right through me. She is clearly in total disbelief that these words are flowing from my mouth. Words flow when there are no borders. Secrets flow when there are no more words to hide them.

"I will tell you right now, Ruby Jane, you will not live in this house and be an abomination to our family and our God! You will not continue to be here and—"

"I don't need your permission to not be here, Momma. I was really never here to begin with," I reply.

We are interrupted by a knock on the door. Momma turns to me. She appears to be completely shocked. I, however, am not. For once, I have located my exit row in advance.

Momma guardedly opens the door.

"Hey, my sweetest baby girl," he says as he enters. "It is so wonderful to see you again."

Momma turns three shades of pale.

"Hi, Uncle Kevin."

He lifts me into his arms and hugs me so tight that my heart feels gift-wrapped in love.

"Are you ready? Your Aunt Francis is waiting in the car. No offense, Susie."

He directs his comments at Momma.

"She doesn't feel comfortable here. But you know that already."

"Let's go, Ruby Jane. We have grand things to do! It was really good to see you, Susie Q. You take care of yourself now, ya hear?"

He leans down and softly kisses Momma on the cheek. Momma reaches her hand up to her cheek as if holding on to a memory that is about to be made. Uncle Kevin grasps my hand tightly and smiles at me with those protective deep blue eyes, and I feel wanted and safe.

As we walk to the car, he lovingly places his hand on my shoulder, leans into my ear, and softly says, "Ruby Jane, I am not sure what is going on, but I don't judge. I never judge."

"I appreciate this so much, Uncle Kevin," I say, and I mean it.

"I am just so glad you called. Now I am here for whatever you need. Oh, and I brought a shovel. You know, just in case."

Chapter 18

AN ANSWERED PRAYER

We drive away, the three of us—me, Uncle Kevin, and Aunt Francis. An odd combination of uncertainty considering I am only seventeen, and my entire life with them has been actually without them, a tactic my momma and daddy attempted to accomplish daily.

We drive and drive and drive. We drive for hours and for days and for lifetimes. This pilgrimage feels to me as unplanned as Kevin's past. I lay my head onto the back of the cool leather seat and close my eyes, and for the first time since the matter of contention revolving around the Unfortunate Lickety-Split incident, I fall into a deep sleep.

*****

When I wake, we appear to be on the infamous God-Only-Knows-Where Tour. God doesn't care about where I go. God gave up on me long ago. I sit up slowly as I rub the sleep from my eyes, as well as from my past. I attempt a small glance through the front windshield.

The road ahead is dark, yet there are half-shaped small circles of lights floating toward us from opposite lanes. Aunt Francis gazes straight ahead. She is not moving. She seems to be looking into her past, her present, her future, and most importantly, MY future.

Until this one moment, I have been exhaustively protected and shielded from these two humans. Secrets have swarmed, rumors have raged, and hushed coffee conversations have been uttered among adults. However, I've been kept in a lifetime of protective silence—a protective silence that will be terminated tonight.

There are moments in our lives when we regret certain decisions. And this one? This one tops the fucking list as the most regrettable decision ever made by mankind.

As I adjust to my newfound surroundings, I hear so calmly and peacefully, "Kevin, I just know that she is the answer to our prayers."

Francis sings this out in an angelic, whispered hush as her long red hair drapes over the seat. Her hair smells of fresh laundry and peppermint bark.

"She has been sent to us, Kevin. She is the answer we have prayed for. God, in his almighty wisdom, has granted us this holy treasure, and we are going to make sure that we…"

She pauses.

"You and me, darlin', we…we use her gifts for us."

I remain silent in the back, as they are both unaware that I have become a part of their conversation. My heart is rushing, and I don't recall my last attempt at this smile covering my body from head to toe. I am over the moon to be an answer to anyone's prayers. I've only known the opposite.

I am not a fan of prayers. They are nothing more than bullshit sentences said aloud to intentionally impress others that your entry into the Kingdom has been sealed. But now? The utter joy I feel to be a part of an answered prayer is indescribable.

We slowly pull into a Gulf gas station, and the car floats next to the pump. Uncle Kevin quiets the engine. It is utter darkness with the exception of a brilliant glow of blue and bright orange from a sign blinking words of comfort for wayward souls.

I feel safe and wrapped in a love I've never known. I know it may sound selfish, but I like being liked. I am wanted, and I am wanted by family, and that makes it even sweeter.

Francis gets out of the car and walks inside the gas station. I sit in peace, reflecting on my new title. An answer! Goddamn! I am an answer! I am no longer the problem.

When Francis returns, she opens the door.

"Ruby," Francis says firmly, "go on in there and get us something to eat. Why, I am half-starved already. Surely you are hungry, baby girl!"

I am taken aback. I have no money. I have left everything behind. I have no more than a flowered small suitcase that is brimming with nothing more than Lifetime movie packing skills in my rush to flee the scene.

"I, uh, well, to be honest, I don't have nothing," I respond.

Francis leans her head toward me and whispers, "Well, I suggest you find a way to get it, child."

Although it is completely dark, her eyes stare through me. I can literally feel a frightening chill overwhelm me inside of the car.

"What do you expect me to do?" I ask.

"What do I expect you to do? Sweet fucking Jesus, Ruby, I expect you to carry your weight, child. You didn't think me and your Uncle Kevin would simply rescue you, and you would just come with us and ride off on our dreams now, baby? Is that what you thought?"

She leans her head toward me in the back seat and darts a devious grin.

"We are all responsible for providing for this family, and you are not excluded just because you are Susie Bitch Q's offspring."

I sit in speechlessness. I don't have a fucking cent to my name. What the actual fuck does she expect of me? I am unglued.

Francis paces around the car. She is restless, and I know enough about life to know that this has been an atrocious decision on my part. She becomes increasingly agitated with me as she rubs her hands together.

I am looking for my exit row. But before I can plan my blueprint, the car door opens, and Francis's hand grabs me, violently pulling me out of the car.

"I ain't tellin' you again, you worthless piece of shit! You stay with us, you pay with us!"

She is screaming like a fucking wild animal, dragging me by my hair and forcing me through the parking lot. It is pitch-black, and there is no help to be found. She jerks me into the restroom and impatiently fastens the lock behind her. She then turns and softens her hair with her palms and inhales a deep, calming breath.

"Now, Ruby Jane, you didn't have to make this so difficult."

She speaks as if she is addressing a much-beloved Sunday school class.

I look around and turn to see a complete stranger, a haggard old man dressed in rugged gray pants and a faded shirt with a Conoco patch sewn above the side pocket. He is smiling at me. His teeth are rotted, and he smells like burned cabbage. His smile is dangerous. It is not a smile that makes me comfortable.

"Ruby, now this here is my friend Jerry. Jerry needs some really special time with you tonight. He is lonely, Ruby, and you and I both know what that must feel like, right?"

Jerry smiles, toothless. The oil in his hair matches the oil on his clothes. I feel vomit rising in my throat. I am afraid. What is happening to me? Is this the answer to the prayer that I am supposed to be?

"Where is Uncle Kevin?" I scream at the top of my lungs. "Where is he!"

"I'll tell you where he is, you selfish bitch!"

She reaches and grabs the back of my neck, pulling it to her face.

"He is out there in this godforsaken world, trying to make things okay for us! He takes care of us! He takes care of us every single day! And it is our job to take care of him!"

Oil Jerry licks his lips and grabs me. He forcefully pushes me to the floor as he unzips his pants and pulls out his dick. My angry, pursed lips are only met with hard slaps to my body, my head, and my legs.

"DO IT!" she screams.

She grabs my head and delivers it to his dick and forces my jaws open as she smirks hysterically. She pounds my head with her fists over and over with full force. The movement of her hand to the back of my neck is now in cadence to the movement of his hips. And then? Then it is over.

I abruptly spit the repulsive liquid out onto the filthy cement floor as I cry and heave hysterically, trying to catch my breath. I see Oil Boy shove Francis a wad of cash, which she hastily shoves into the side pocket of her jacket. I can't help but wonder how much I am worth.

Oil Boy quietly leaves the bathroom, but not without glaring at me, leaning down toward the floor and spitting in my face. I endure my pathetic position on the floor. My mouth is seasoned with the brutal taste of come, blood, and rage. The anger overpowers me.

"Well, would you look at you, baby girl. You finally have figured out how to make your own way in this world. You are a shining star! You just wait! We are gonna do great things in the name of God! Praise be, baby girl. Great, holy things. Welcome to our family."

She leaves me on the floor, damaged and alone. Scraps. I remain completely still as sobs rack my body. Eventually, I am able to crawl into a stall and close the door behind me.

In the stall, I am face-to-face with the scum and waste left to me. It doesn't offend me. I find comfort in situations that remind me of who I really am. It seems most appropriate for my life right now. There are no tears. There is only me, alone.

I reach for my hair, slowly twisting what is left from my scalp, a scalp that is throbbing from Francis's repeated blows.

My solitary confinement is interrupted by the opening of the door. I hear heavy boots traipsing across the floor, and then I smell the familiar oil as it penetrates my nostrils. I carefully peek through the stall door and see Oil Boy standing in front of the sink.

He rubs his fingers through his hair and checks what teeth he has left in the mirror. He begins to whistle a most familiar tune. What is it? I cannot put a name to the melody. He leisurely removes the thick leather belt from his waist, wraps it around his arm, tightens it with his teeth, and casually pulls a needle from his back pocket. He is no longer whistling.

I sit back, only to observe. He seats himself on the floor and works to make himself comfortable. He then places the needle against his arm and plunges it deep into his flesh. Immediately, his eyes dramatically roll into the back of his head.

His smile erupts gradually and slowly as the drug overtakes his entire body. He takes a deep breath and rests his head against the cement wall. I am almost jealous of how happy he appears. I deserve this kind of feeling too.

When I am sure that he is completely heroin happy, I open the door and step out of the stall. He doesn't move. Is he dead? I kick his boot for a reaction. He still does not move.

I cautiously but effortlessly lean over and remove the belt from around his arm. I then strap it so delicately around his neck as if he is adorned by a charming noose necklace. And then? I pull. I pull with everything that could possibly be in me. I pull with fury, with resentment, with outrage.

Oil Boy's eyes shoot wide open in panic and shock. Both of his hands suddenly jerk up and grasp my arms as he fights to remove the belt from around his neck. He kicks his feet violently and reaches for any part of my body that will help free him from my hold. But my will is stronger than his. My will is powered by secrets and memories.

And when he no longer moves and I am certain that his pathetic life has left this world, I callously drop the belt. The buckle clinks as it lands on the bathroom floor. I brace myself against the wall and attempt to catch my breath.

My blood is soaring through my veins, and my body is shaking from the adrenaline. I feel alive. My heart pumping out of my chest feels invigorating. It validates that I am still standing. Oil Boy lies sprawled out across the floor with a slight trickle of crimson-red blood dripping from his nose. I step over his body, kicking him one last time, because he deserves it.

Before I leave, I bend down to his ear and whisper, "Tell Granddaddy Tuesday I said hi."

And then I spit in his face.

I courageously walk back to the car, my head held high and my confidence even higher. Fuck-Face Francis is seated in the front seat, discreetly awaiting our departure. She doesn't dare speak to me. I open the door and slide into the back while sneering in her direction just in case she contemplates glancing my way.

Uncle Kevin cheerfully hops in the car, absolutely unaware of any event that has transpired during our unremarkable gas-up. He leans back to me and affectionately hands me an ice-cold Pepsi and a Pixy Stix the size of Texas in a long, striped plastic tube.

He lovingly reaches out to me and ruffles the only hair I haven't twisted away and says, "I sure do love you. Uncle Kevin is here. I am so glad you called. Whatever you need? You just ask me and Aunt Francis."

"I really appreciate you, Uncle Kevin. I'm not sure what I would have done without you. Oh, and you too, Francis!" I add in an over-euphoric, exaggerated tone. "Momma always said that you were a true gem, Aunt Francis."

She turns to glare at me as if demanding that I shut up.

"Did she now?" Uncle Kevin responds in a tone as if challenging the truth to that statement. "Well, she sure is a gem, Ruby. You know what? You were actually named after a gem, Ruby. Your momma named you after the crimson-blood-stained cross where our Christ was crucified for our sins. Isn't that something so very special?"

"Huh. You don't say," I reply.

My mind reflects to the trickle of crimson-red blood running from Oil Boy's nose—ruby red, to be exact. Ah, "Stayin' Alive!" Yes, that's it. That's the song I couldn't remember earlier. How ironic is that? I just love Andy Gibb Jesus.

*****

Detroit. Detroit. That is where the much-anticipated final destination of our cross-country adventure lands us exactly six days after the gas station Complimentary Noose Incident.

"I have something to say," Uncle Kevin addresses us over morning breakfast. "I have been praying so hard and talking to God, and he has finally answered me. God has directed us to the Divine of the Righteous Congregation," Uncle Kevin boldly announces at the Waffle House breakfast table.

I pick at the watery scrambled eggs while Francis allocates her time fixing her hair with her only visual—a small pink Mary Kay compact mirror.

"We have been called to spread his Word. We have been summoned to witness to the sinners and to convert those who face eternal damnation," he concludes. "And in return, the congregation has graciously awarded us a parsonage in exchange."

Francis is thrilled, and she childishly claps her hands.

"A parsonage! How wonderful, Kevin. I am so proud of you, our dear, godly leader. Our very own parsonage. Now, Ruby, isn't that just something?"

I wonder if there will be forced blow jobs in exchange for dollar bills at the parsonage.

"Oh, Kevin, I am so excited. Now when do we get to see it?" Francis continues. "I've always wanted a home, one that I can make my very own."

She stares away from her pancakes dreamily.

"Well, the congregation awaits as I speak. We are headed for great things, and I just know all of the stars have aligned and fulfilled our much-needed purpose. Now are y'all ready?"

Uncle Kevin abruptly stands from his chair and grabs the check from the table. We all know what this means: we get up from the table and walk toward the front entrance of the restaurant.

On command, Uncle Kevin flings himself violently to the ground, grabbing his neck and screaming in gut-wrenching pain.

"My neck! My neck!"

A crowd hurriedly surrounds him and investigates his possible injuries. He writhes and twists and turns in agony, all while Fuck-Face Francis screams in horror.

"You incompetent imbeciles!" she bellows at the professional staff of the Waffle House as she hurriedly collects random phone numbers, workers' names from greasy badges, and expert witness testimony.

I sit back, silently witnessing the fourth Waffle House Academy Award performance in six days. Critique? Quite impressive and hugely entertaining. Semi-Oscar worthy. Three and a half stars.

Uncle Kevin departs in the much-anticipated ambulance while Francis and I follow him to the local hospital, where we will depart with hopes of a fat check and neck brace number four for Uncle Kevin.

As Francis and I wait in the ER parking lot, a dense lull lingers in the air. It makes it near impossible to breathe. We have not spoken to each other since the Unfortunate Noose Incident.

"Ahem."

She coughs uncomfortably and mechanically adjusts the rear-view mirror.

"Listen, this may be a good time to talk about what happened."

"I disagree."

She turns wildly to me and says, "I don't know who the fuck you think you are. But rest assured, your family has been nothing but horrible to me and your Uncle Kevin. I don't like you, Ruby Jane Clancy. Never have. Never will!"

She spits words directly in my face.

"I actually fucking hate you. Your Uncle Kevin is a real good man, I tell you. He has been nothing but good to me, but he is too stupid to see the real truth. For the love of fucking God, I have no idea why Kevin puts any effort into your worthless family. And for some reason, he thinks you hung the actual moon. But God as my witness, I am already working to get you the fuck out of here, you worthless, stupid piece of shit!"

"Really?" I respond. "That is so interesting. I could say the same. I am already working to get you the fuck out of here, you worthless, stupid piece of shit!"

She raises her hand abruptly and slaps me across the face so hard that my right temple slams into the car window.

"How dare you talk to me that way!" she screams. "How dare you!"

"I hate you, and I hate God even more. And you know what? The only thing God did right was not giving you fucking kids!" I scream at the top of my lungs.

The car door opens unexpectedly, and Uncle Kevin blissfully slides into the back seat with a neck brace enveloping his neck and a small black splint on his right arm. The splint is a first. I am so proud of him and this new feature.

"Well, my two favorite ladies, how are you? What a beautiful evening."

"Oh, my sweet Kevin. Why, Ruby Jane and I were just bonding and really learning about each other. She is a fine young lady, Kevin. A fine young lady, I tell you. She already feels like the daughter we always wanted."

"That is wonderful to hear. Let's go. The parsonage is waiting. I am so blessed to have you both in my life right now," Kevin concedes.

"I agree, Uncle Kevin. I am so blessed to especially have found Francis. Wait, Aunt Francis," I say, placing literal sarcastic emphasis on the word *aunt*.

"I sure hope they have a garden at the parsonage, Uncle Kevin. You know how much I love gardening. I actually would like to plant my very own Jesus Saves Garden, just like Grandma's."

"Oh, that is the sweetest thing anyone has ever said. I sure miss my momma. And I'm sure you miss your momma too, but sometimes, life guides you to make changes and to discover a new path. And if that is what you want, Ruby? Then we will make that happen for you. Some of my best memories of my life were spent in my momma's garden. Lots of memories there. Lots I left behind, buried deep in that garden."

His words gradually fade away.

"I have it pictured all in my mind, Uncle Kevin. I will grow roses and strawberries just like Grandma, and I will paint those small wood signs with her favorite scriptures."

My own heart is softening as Grandma's memory spreads into my mind.

"Aunt Francis can help me. It might do us good to spend time together."

WEEDS THROUGH THE FLOORBOARDS

She darts flames in my direction.

Kevin bends his head back toward the back seat and lets out a roar.

"That's a fine idea, Ruby Jane. A fine idea! What can I do to help?"

"Well, for sure, I'm gonna need my very own shovel. Ya know, so I can bury shit too."

I stare dead set into Francis's eyes. I am not sure what I see. However, it looks like fear. Good.

Uncle Kevin's face lights up like an adorned Christmas tree, and he smiles.

"Well, I'll tell ya something real important, Ruby Jane. There's only two things you need in life. One, you need the Word of Christ in your life to help you handle your battles and your problems. And two, you gotta have a shovel to bury those problems you can't handle. Jesus solves battles. Shovels solve problems."

Understood.

Chapter 19

OH DANNY BOY

The Promised Land Parsonage is more or less a run-down six-hundred-square-foot trailer located next to a barely functioning, dilapidated building in South Detroit. There exists no heat or AC, but in all fairness, rent does not exist as well. Rent is to be paid with Uncle Kevin's Considering-Delivering Package Deal. We consider them to be sinners damned to the fire, and we deliver them from the fire. It's as easy as that.

There are eighty-seven congregants who have feverishly prayed for our arrival. Eighty-seven congregants anxiously await our endeavors to save not only the world but also the dwindling population of the Divine of the Righteous Congregation.

Uncle Kevin is a fucking rock star in the Band of Jesus due to his claim to fame as being the human who discovered Noah's Ark and the Ark of the Covenant. His multiple prophetic digs for deity and biblical discoveries in Israel have landed him into Holy Trinity celebrity status within the community.

After many days on the Highway to Hell Tour, we finally arrive at the parsonage on a Thursday with nothing more than what can be held in one suitcase each and a trunk burdened with Neck Braces for Humanity.

Brother Lloyd, an old man in his sixties, furiously waves us down with both hands as we pull in from the highway. His efforts remind me of one of those blowups at the used car sale lots—50-percent discount per soul for every soul you save.

Uncle Kevin responds to this seemingly overdramatic welcome by calmly rolling the window down and awaiting his accolades of greatness.

Brother Lloyd leans into the car.

"Oh, Brother Kevin, we are eternally blessed in his precious name to have you and your beautiful family here to serve. What an honor in Christ. A true honor. We have prayed and prayed for you. And, well, here you are, our answer. Oh, forgive me."

He laughs and moves from our path.

"Oh, and please, you can park in the back."

He points his entire body toward the back of the building.

"I really hate to rush you, seein' as you just got here and all, but we have some work that needs tending to kind of immediately, if you don't mind too much."

"Of course," Kevin replies.

Brother Lloyd rushes to meet us in the back, where he proudly escorts us around the church grounds. There is a paved walkway that forms a trail leading to the front of the building. I notice several small patches of worn grass, a perfect place for my Jesus Saves Garden.

There are small steps leading to the main entrance that remind me of step-on-a-crack-break-your-momma's-back commitments. I would be lying if I say I try my hardest to not step on the crack. I miss Momma.

I cautiously step inside and take a deep breath. The church enlightens my senses of my home. There are things you smell in a church that no one prepares you for—the smell of aging old wood from pews that have an urgency to support you and onion leaf pages in a hymnal with musical notes matching words that we've yet to sing. Dammit, it feels like home.

This church embraces me with a sense of familiarity and routine, and for the first moment since leaving, I miss home. I miss Momma, Dixie, and Slideshow Wednesdays. I miss Netti and Betty.

I release my breath and open my eyes. There is a weathered brown piano to the left of the aisle, a small lectern in the middle, and a heartfelt cadence in my soul as I walk the aisle. This is where I come from. This is who I am.

My attention is immediately focused to the front of the room. On full display in all its grandeur lies a bountiful floral arrangement that graciously spreads itself by stretching across the entire altar. My nostrils fill with vibrant fragrances that float all the way to where I stand. Stargazer lilies, roses, carnations, lilacs, and peonies—their aromas embrace me with peace and overwhelm me with memories. Momma used to say that a song remembers when, and I could say the same about a smell. The aroma of the church takes me back to Pine Creek.

I slowly approach the extravagant arrangement, calculating my impending efforts to transport these incredible botanicals to my very own Jesus Saves Garden. I effortlessly reach down to pluck a stargazer to my nose. Then my own gaze lands on what appears to be a tiny human hand that happens to be attached to a small human body.

I scream, leap back, and read the room for help. Where is the exit row?

My scream startles all present parties, which leads Brother Lloyd to jump to attention as he barrels down the aisle, racing to me, with Uncle Kevin quickly following. Brother Lloyd reaches the end of the aisle, where I am standing horrified and unwilling to negotiate a reason as to what has just happened.

"Oh, now don't you worry yourself. This here is Danny. He is harmless, Ruby. There's no need to be afraid or alarmed. Why, he is just simply here, waiting to be resurrected."

Upon hearing this, Fuck-Face Francis rushes her entire body to the altar and dramatically falls to her knees. She raises her hands to the sky and cries out in multiple unknown languages. She displays the signs of the cross backward and forward. She passive-aggressively

WEEDS THROUGH THE FLOORBOARDS

touches Danny's head, his arms, and his feet. She prays aloud, alone, and silently. But she does not fool me.

We all know the truth. Oh Danny Boy is dead—deader than dead. I understand that Uncle Kevin is thrilled about his current expedition, but I also know he is digging through his trunk right now, looking for his shovel.

I wonder if I should suggest someone relocate Oh Danny Boy to somewhere other than here, because if truth be told, there is no amount of stargazer lilies that can mask the potential smell of Oh Danny Boy's pipes that are no longer calling.

*****

I am not allowed to sleep in the parsonage. There is no room for me. There is no room for me anywhere on this earth. I have no place. I do not belong. I am once again finding myself envious of Swan-Dive Betty. All I want is to belong. I promise that one day, I will make that happen.

I am given the keys to the storage shed in the backyard. The shed. I may not be worthy of the kingdom of heaven, but I sure as shit am worthy of a backyard shed that looks like you need a tetanus shot if you enter.

There is no bed. There is, however, an oversized wooden workbench that will easily accommodate my weary body. The sides of the bench are splintered and jagged, much like my life. An overwhelming, strong smell of gasoline infiltrates throughout the decrepit space, which turns the simple task of lighting a cigarette into a frightening game of Russian roulette.

Fuck-Face Francis has provided several blankets and soft pillows laid neatly over the wooden workbench. At first, I imagined this kind gesture might appear as a truce. It is only when I see the enormous leftover, half-dead flowers from Old Danny Boy's Altar Display sitting on the grimy window ledge that I realize this is not a truce but a warning.

*****

111

It is night three of our arrival at the Divine of the Righteous Congregation in Detroit. It is Wednesday. We have yet to attend a service, which means tonight is Uncle Kevin's red carpet premiere.

He is properly introduced by Brother Lloyd, who reads a résumé worthy of a sitting US president. And as Uncle Kevin takes the podium, the entire congregation jumps to their feet, clapping and sincerely welcoming him into the fold—or the cult, as I prefer.

I am seated in the very back row, surveying the audience in efforts of finding the one human fuckup that belongs with me. I randomly take their inventory and judge them one by one.

The worship service is inundated with screaming, wailing, singing, jumping, foreign tongues, and snakes; and yet Oh Danny Boy's body is nowhere to be seen. I reckon the resurrection has stood him up like a bad date.

And then it happens. I see her. It's actually true what they say about lesbians who cannot be lesbians. We see one another—not in the visual sense but in the emotional sense. We truly see one another without words. We see one another trapped and buried in guilt and grief. But others cannot see us. They don't understand.

She walks up directly to me at the close of the last hymn. She leans over the pew and gently brings her face to mine.

"Welcome, Ruby. We are so glad to have your family here. It's been a long time since we've had someone new. My name is Lisa."

Lisa is tall, her long brown hair touches her waist, and she is wearing a dark-chocolate dress that matches her eyes perfectly. She warmly extends her hand, which I grasp and shake.

"It's nice to meet you, Lisa. I, well, I am new here, and I don't know anyone, and I—"

She immediately cuts me off and interrupts, saying, "Oh, I just simply cannot imagine, Ruby. That's why I wanted to make sure I met you. Everyone needs someone here. I know you are new and don't know anyone. It must be hard."

I don't respond.

"I have an idea," she finally replies. "Let's go out for a walk. I can show you around town and introduce you to some of my friends."

"That would be nice. Thank you," I reply gratefully.

We leave the church and enter into the night, strolling side by side in silence. Something about Lisa makes me feel known and protected.

"So, Ruby, I am really glad you are here."

She pulls out a pack of cigarettes from the pocket of her skirt and lights one, then delicately hands it to me.

"Thanks," I say, placing it up to my lips. "So where are we headed?"

She leans into my ear and softly whispers, "Wherever you want, Ruby. But I believe in choices, so I am actually going to offer you options."

"Um, all right," I respond with complete uncertainty about where this conversation is heading.

"Option A: we can continue our fake walk through town, and I can help in saving your lost soul from eternal damnation. That's what we do, right? Save lost souls? Recruit others for Christ at all times?"

I nod my head in total agreement and complete understanding. I like New Lisa.

"Option B," she continues, "we can just get totally fucked up."

I am stunned by this option, as she is literally standing over me like Laura Ingalls in *Little House on the Prairie* attire.

"I'm listening," I reply, anxiously awaiting the next option.

"Or C, which is personally my favorite, we can fuck."

She seductively reaches out for my hand, places it to her lips, and bites down…hard. I don't flinch. Pain feels good.

"You are a smart girl, Ruby. I knew the moment I saw you. Since we are going to hell, we might as well earn it."

Go big or go home. And just like that, Detroit is not so bad.

Chapter 20

SHED SEX

I openly propose this question honestly and ask only that one have thoughtful consideration before pondering an appropriate response. What is better than sex? Shed sex. Shed sex is better than non-shed sex.

I am thoroughly unaware of how it is that New Lisa Upton magically appears in my life without warning or notice. But rest assured, she makes me come every thirty minutes, all day, every day.

New Lisa Upton is incredibly angry at everyone, every human and everything other than human, and she takes this anger out on my clit. She makes me scream. She makes me cry. She makes me care. She makes me not care. She is like an uncontrollable, raging fire that is dangerous to touch but even more dangerous to ignore.

We spend our days completely naked in my makeshift shed-bed, laughing, drinking, smoking weed, and experiencing so many orgasms I think my fucking brain will explode. We walk daily to the Howard Johnson's, where New Lisa's brother, Jimmy, works as a front office clerk.

WEEDS THROUGH THE FLOORBOARDS

We play for hours in the small wannabe gym on the first floor. Lisa ties weights around her ankles and attempts to run on the treadmill at its highest speed, which makes me bowl over in fits of laughter. I spin balls to the wall on the stationary bike as if I am trying to get away from everything and everyone.

We calmly lounge by the crystal-blue pool and order grilled cheese sandwiches with pickles and french fries. The delivery of such food arrives with snow-white cloth napkins that appear perfectly creased and firmly starched with a faint smell of pressed lemons.

I've never been allowed to swim, which makes the Howard Johnson's pool to be the ultimate of luxuries. I don't navigate the deep end, but I do submerge my entire body in the shallow end. The pool is inviting and washes away our sins, our worries, and our secrets.

We spend our evenings in church, praying for lost souls and pretend-crying through Uncle Kevin's moving and poignant sermons, which call others to the altar for reformation and condemnation. We actively praise and worship and shout out loud to whoever may hear us, but New Lisa and I both know we are shouting out and praising to thank God in heaven that we didn't die during our last fuck session. It is that intense.

The best part is that we literally have no love for each other. There is nothing but desire and lust. We love others but not each other. The two of us don't belong anywhere. No one wants us. Scraps.

We share intimate secrets and future hopes. I share Granddaddy Tuesdays, and New Lisa shares that her stepdad, Buddy, did the same thing, except on Saturdays, when her momma was at the Women's Quilting Club down at the local community center.

I promise her I will kill Buddy if I ever find him, and she promises to be there for me no matter what. I like the comfort that brings to me. It's like a soft blanket of protection that covers your entire being. Team Ruby.

New Lisa Upton is a hollow shell, and what shell is left on the outside is shattered and broken. This is why we connect. This was how she knew to walk up to me the very first night we met. This is how we know that we love those whom God does not allow us to love. This is how we know that we will never be okay. This is how we understand that we are not seen.

And on the twenty-third day in Detroit, New Lisa Upton silently wades into the turquoise hues of the pool at the Howard Johnson's with the wannabe gym's weights attached to her waist. She leaves a haphazardly scribbled note on a wadded-up napkin next to her unfinished fries that reads, "Can you see me now?" We bury New Lisa Upton the following Wednesday.

Uncle Kevin stands poignantly at the head of the congregation and emphatically reads scripture about the beauty of life after death and how New Lisa is finally home. The rain is coming down in burdensome sheets. Thunder claps, and the sky twinkles with bolts of lightning. I wonder if New Lisa is sending me a sign. I wonder if she is with Swan-Dive Betty. I am bitter and completely heartbroken—not because New Lisa Upton is gone but because I wasn't fucking invited.

*****

I am lying in my shed, listening to the sounds of the world waking up and unfolding around me. It is quiet and serene, but not for long.

The porch door to the parsonage creaks loudly and slams against the siding of the trailer, and screaming commences, filling the atmosphere. I immediately leap to the window and wipe the grit with my forearm to observe what is happening.

"Don't think you can walk into my house and take what is not yours!" Fuck-Face Francis yells at the top of her lungs.

She is running feverishly toward the shed.

"I will do whatever I want, you fucking cunt! I told you to stay out of my way, or I will stab you right in the face!"

Oh, sweetest, dear baby Jesus, I know what is about to happen.

The shed door violently swings open.

"Get your ass in the car! Now!"

Dixie solidly points to the direction of the street.

WEEDS THROUGH THE FLOORBOARDS

"NOW!" she screams louder as if doing so will make it happen faster.

Hearing the commotion, Uncle Kevin awkwardly sprints down the sidewalk from the church.

"Wait just a minute now, Dixie. You better just hold up right there, young lady. You are not taking her anywhere," he argues calmly as I stand still, glancing from one to the other, unsure of what team I should join.

"You better not come any closer, Kevin. I will personally bury you with your own shovel! You cannot take this child away from her mother and expect me to not bring her home! Can you? Do you have any idea what Susie is going through?"

"You get off my property now!" Francis screams.

"Your property?"

Dixie laughs harshly.

"You better hear me, and hear me good! If you think for one minute that I give two shits about going to jail in return for beating your ass, well, you done lost your mind! Don't forget who you are fucking with! Jail is a fucking vacation!"

I reluctantly follow Dixie to the car, leaning over my shoulder, only to see Francis's smartass smirk and the nodding of her head in secret approval of Dixie's crazed ambush.

I open the car door and slide in quietly. Dixie jumps into the car and squeals out of the parking lot in a dramatic scene worthy of *The Dukes of Hazzard*.

"Have you lost your ever-loving mind?" she finally asks. "Your momma has been sick with fear and nonstop worry since you left. How could you do this to her? You haven't called, not a fucking word. No one knew where you went. Are you even listening to me?"

I stare straight ahead, speechless.

"Answer me!"

Again, I assert my Fifth Amendment privilege and turn my head to rest against the window.

"Okay, look, I know you hate me for what happened, and I really don't blame you. I was stupid and drunk and high, and I shoulda never crawled in bed with Netti.

"But, Ruby, are you gonna tell me that you ain't never done nothing that you really, really regret? You ain't never made one bad decision that you will never forgive yourself for? 'Cause if you say no, I just don't believe you. Everyone makes—"

I cut her off.

"What do you care? What do you care what I think? You know how I feel about Netti, and you just up and fucked her? How am I supposed to not care?"

Dixie timidly chews on the bottom of her lip. She clears her throat.

"Ahem. Well, hate me all ya want. Stand in the fucking line. Get on the waitlist. I'm used to it. It don't bother me one fucking bit. Ain't none of this about me. There is another reason I am here, Ruby Jane. I didn't drive all this way to give two shits about how you feel about me. There's something I need to tell you."

My heart drops.

"Whatever. Just say it already," I reply.

"It's your momma, Ruby Jane. She's real sick. She is asking to see ya. That's why I'm here."

"What do you mean sick? She got the flu or something? You could have just called," I finally say.

"It's cancer, Ruby. It came fast, and it came strong, and it is taking her quickly. She wants to see you, so I promised her I would find you. And when Dixie Anne Thomas makes a promise, she fucking keeps it."

"By the way, how did you find me?" I inquire.

"Girl, don't be stupid. Were you born in a box? Your Uncle Kevin is an actual walking, talking idiot. He literally calls me twice, sometimes three times a week asking for money, asking for favors. That's what he does. He cons people. He gets their trust and wins them over with his saintly sermons and his divine revelations. And then when he knows he can run? He runs.

"And that bitch Francis? He don't love her—never did and never will. He is just smart enough to know that having a pretend God-fearing wife on his side wins a lot of faith in his corner. But I will tell you this, Ruby Jane. Your Uncle Kevin is batshit and downright dangerous. Hell, they both are. You should, quite frankly, thank me for showing up today.

"And your momma has been worried about his influence on you. All he has ever done is scam church after church after church. It won't be long until Detroit is his next victim. Now, I'm taking you home, and that is all we're gonna say about that. You hear me?"

"So let me get this straight. Momma is worried about Uncle Kevin's influence on me, yet she sent YOU to pick me up? Now that's solid."

"Shut up. I do just fine by our family. I know I ain't perfect, but when it comes to family? I am there."

"Yeah, there as in literally fucking my girlfriend," I respond.

"Oh, grow the fuck up! You are only seventeen. You don't know nothing about having a girlfriend—or even a black boyfriend at that! You don't know nothing about relationships," she says.

"Me? Seriously? You are lecturing me about relationships, Dixie? For fuck's sake, your last boyfriend ended up in a freezer!" I shout, defending myself.

She looks over to me, leans her head back, and bursts into a fit of laughter.

She continues as she laughs through her words.

"You got that right, and don't you forget it. Don't piss me off, Ruby Jane, not ever. I got a brand-new Kenmore with last month's welfare check, and I ain't afraid to use it."

I am horrified by her complete and utter lack of empathy. But I look back at her and burst into a fit of laughter too.

"Oh, my sweet Ruby Jane," she says gently as she reaches across the seat for my hand.

She grabs and squeezes tight.

"I've missed you something terrible. I love you more than anything, and I really am sorry. I promise to never fuck your girlfriends ever again—unless you start dating that Farrah Fawcett actress. Then it's all bets off. I would definitely fuck her."

I smile back.

"I missed you too, Dixie. You are a fucking bitch, but I've missed ya."

We have been driving for countless miles in comfortable silence when she turns to me and randomly blurts out, "Besides, Netti is a lousy fuck. You really need to get around more."

And after my New Lisa Shed Sex Bed romps, I could not agree more.

Chapter 21

HUMPTY DUMPTY

We encounter an extensive drive for what seems like countless days, finally arriving home. Home. It doesn't feel like home. Home is where you belong. I don't belong here. I don't belong anywhere.

Dixie pulls slowly into the driveway, which is entirely overwhelmed with cars. It's a parking lot full of deathbed escorts.

"Ruby Jane, listen to me, baby," Dixie says softly. "Your momma is...well...she is comfortable, but she is not well. I just want you to be prepared when you go in and see her. Now I know you ain't been gone long, but she has really declined. This cancer came long ago, but your momma didn't want to alarm anyone, and she didn't want anyone fussing over her. You know how she gets."

I don't know what to do with these words. What the fuck does this actually mean? Why isn't she in the hospital? Has she even seen a doctor?

I cautiously open the front door, peeking into the unexpected. The smells of my childhood envelop and embrace my entire body. And just like how churches have familiar smells, home has a smell too; and today, my home smells of death. After the twenty-nine-day Detroit Tour of Devastation I've been on, I just want to be somewhere. But this somewhere is not my place.

I step inside, where I am immediately greeted by numerous congregation members, many of whom are on bended knee, raising praise to the one and only Jesus What's-His-Fucking-Name. The first bride of Christ who greets me is mean old Sister Wilma with a stick shoved so far up her fucking ass I want to pull it out and choke her with it. But then I would feel sorry for her, because as far as I know, the only thing that has ever been stuck in her is that stick up her ass.

Sister Wilma is the first to speak.

"Well, my goodness gracious! Would you lookie here! We welcome you back, Ruby. We prayed for you all day every day that God would direct the path you are on. It's just so good to see you. There is forgiveness, Ruby. I do need to tell you that God's kingdom is here right now in this house, and by golly, we are gonna raise up your momma. But on no account of you being sinful and deceitful and..."

I physically push her to the side and shove past her.

"Fuck off," I whisper to her under my breath, making sure she hears me.

She dramatically clutches her chest as if I have put a bullet in it.

I walk straight into Momma's room. Her face lights up when she sees me; however, her eyes are dark, her skin is darker, and I know. She looks so tiny in that big bed. The quilts my grandma sewed us swallow her whole.

"Hey, Momma," I whisper softly as I sit next to her and cradle her in my arms.

"Hey back, Ruby Jane, my sweet Ruby Jane. I am so glad you came home. I am so happy."

She looks at me, smiling from ear to ear. She is so beautiful when she smiles.

Dixie has followed me into the bedroom and joins us on the bed.

"Thank you, Dixie," Momma says to her.

This may be the most intimate moment I have ever witnessed between the two of them.

"Ruby Jane," Momma continues, "there are some things I need to say."

"No, Momma, you don't need to say anything."

I try to put an end to what is coming.

"God is calling me home, Ruby Jane. I am finally going home to my sweet Beulah Land. I wanted to make sure to see your face once more."

"Momma, don't say that. Don't talk like that. Have you seen a doctor? Have you taken—"

"Shhh. Don't you dare bother yourself with all that nonsense. You know that is not what we do, Ruby. We depend on God. God is our physician, not man. There is no other way but his way."

She looks so peaceful as she speaks.

"Momma, I am sorry. I just didn't know what to do, and…"

"Ruby Jane."

She takes my hand and holds it tight to her cheek.

"Don't. I need you to listen to me right now. I am leaving, baby. I am going to a better place. But you? You are going to hell. You better make amends for all your ways of unrighteousness. Or, child, you will burn in the eternal lakes of hell, and we will never see each other again. You hear me? Not me or your daddy."

"Why did you send Dixie for me, Momma? Is this what you wanted to say to me? Is this why Dixie came all the way to Detroit? I thought you wanted to see me, Momma. But you don't see me, because you won't see me for who I am, for what I am, for who God made me!" I cry.

"Ruby Jane, just stop all that nonsense. Do you want to spend your eternity burning in hell? Is that what you want?" she says.

"No, Momma. Hell doesn't scare me. I've been living in it my whole life. I ain't scared. They know me there. Goodbye, Momma. I love you."

I slowly bend down and sweetly kiss her on the cheek, knowing this will be the last time, and then I walk away. I walk away from it all.

*****

Momma died at seven thirty-eight the very next morning.

We bury Momma on a Tuesday next to Daddy at the Ellsworth Cemetery on Canaan Road, behind the skating rink, facing east. As we lower her body into the ground, I feel a strong embrace on my shoulder and a voice in my ear.

"We are here to help."

"Hey, Uncle Kevin," I say.

I look for the exit row. I can only see Dixie, smoking a Pall Mall and sipping the drink of the month out of a shiny silver flask. And leaning against the car is Aunt Francis, signaling to me the utmost fuck-you smoke signals coming from within her soul. People who say that life cannot get any worse than what it is right now have never met Fuck-Face Francis.

Life is always and forever going to be worse than you think it ever will be. Trust me. I am Ruby Jane Clancy, and right now? I am officially an orphan. It's okay. I've always been an orphan, just not the kind people think of.

There is an after-funeral gathering at the church, a typical and predictable routine of the Kingdom. They are like clockwork in any and all situations involving dead people. Sister Smithson organizes the buffet line, filled with homemade casseroles and desserts that will last all summer long if needed. Sister Darla is swatting children's hands that grasp for the cookies as they run and squeal and laugh, chasing one another around the room, completely oblivious to why we are gathered. They are just happy because they belong.

Brother Rogers approaches me with a tedious, grim look on his face. I would like to think I know what is coming, but I know nothing anymore.

"Ruby, we have thought over it, we have prayed over it, and we have suffered long and hard over it. We feel like the best outcome from this most terrible situation is for you to come to our flock. You belong here. We will make sure you have everything you need. But in return, you must give us what we need."

I pause in total silence. What they need?

"What exactly are you saying?" I innocently ask.

"Well..."

He looks around the room to witness anyone who might be listening.

"You repent with an open and honest heart. You repent of the shame you have brought upon our name, openly and publicly. You must repent. And in return, your Uncle Kevin is gonna move in with you and help you get on your feet."

I have a sudden urge to vomit. Get on my feet? Fuck-Face Francis just had me on my knees, sucking dick at a Detroit truck stop. This cannot be happening.

"You really don't have other options. It's either the church or foster care. You have another year until you are of age, and we both know foster care is not the place for children. That system is often broken. You will be so much better off with real family."

"First of all, I am not a child," I reply. "And second, I don't want to stay with Uncle Kevin. You don't understand. I want to stay with my Aunt Dixie. Has anyone talked to her? She is where I belong."

"Don't be foolish, Ruby Jane. You are still a child in the eyes of the law, and your Aunt Dixie left us ages ago. She ain't fit to raise a hamster, all strung out on the devil's grass and liquid of the demons. She is unworthy to even attempt to raise a child."

"I disagree," I confirm with a look in my eye that would strike one of their sermon serpents dead. "She is good to me, better than anyone else in my life. She means well, and she loves and cares for me, which is far more than I can say for all you. You...you are all hypocrites acting like you are all perfect. You don't know nothing about me!"

I am causing an actual scene at this point. Sister Hazeline comes barreling toward me and puts her hand up as if she will knock the reckoning into the seat of my pants.

"Now you listen up, little girl. We all know that you have been through some difficult times, but you will not be disrespectful in his house. And furthermore, you will not continue to blaspheme his name and our congregational family at this respectful gathering. You should be ashamed of yourself. At your own momma's funeral!"

I am at a loss. I am the only one who is for me. Team Ruby. Not one person in this room supports me, loves me, understands me, and wants to help me.

"Well, I reckon you are right, Sister Hazeline, and I would like to offer an apology," I say as I turn to address the entire room.

"Now that's more like it," Sister Hazeline confirms.

"I am sorry. I am truly sorry, and I mean that with every ounce of honesty in my God-given bones."

This emotional statement is met with audible "Thank you Jesuses" and "Grace be to Gods" and "Thanks be to you, our Lord and Saviors."

"I am sorry I fucked a black boy and spilled out his child on the high school gymnasium floor. I am sorry that Sister Wanda's old, decrepit husband found it in his heart to fuck me as a seven-year-old child, and she refused to rescue me. I am sorry I went to your Jesus bullshit rehab, and my sweet Betty dove from the top of the building to escape all of you. I am sorry that I am in love with Annette and want to marry her!"

Their eyes are darting furiously around the room to observe the horrified faces of all the congregants.

"Yes, your Annette. I am sorry God created me this way, much less at all. I am sorry I am still alive right now, so alive that all of you feel some sort of sick need to give a shit about me. But most of all? I feel sorry for all of you, each and every one. I'm leaving now, and I know where I am going, and it ain't here with any of you."

Before I close the door behind me, I turn and add my last jab.

"Oh, and if any of you didn't notice or even care to notice, your beloved youth minister over there? Robbie Sam?"

I point dramatically and directly at his face.

"He really likes to fuck little girls in the back of his car during revivals. He ain't even that good, if truth be told. Maybe y'all wanna pray about that? Just a suggestion. He really needs to learn how to fuck better. I will write it down and put in the suggestion box on my way out."

WEEDS THROUGH THE FLOORBOARDS

At this point, Sister Hazeline faints solidly to the floor. Go big or go home.

*****

I lie silent and completely still on the couch at Dixie's. It is all encompassing in the darkest pitch of blackness, much like my soul.

It has been four days since Momma's In-The-Sweet-By-And-By Service. There is a steady in and out of congregants, elders, pastors, and All Jehovah Praise Be bodies moving about that makes me feel like I live in the fast-food drive-through at the Taco Villa on Fourth Street. Clearly, my Emmy-worthy speech after the funeral had no effect on their efforts to care for the living people whom the dead people leave behind.

They bring casseroles covered in weird-colored cheeses, Crock-Pots holding what is certain to be The God Cure, and enough cakes and homemade pies to make IHOP seem insignificant in the world. That will never happen. I love IHOP.

Their voices carry shushes whenever I am near, and their eyes hold nothing but pity toward me, the orphan. They are trying to change my past by controlling my future.

Uncle Kevin and Fuck-Face Francis have graciously and most uninvitedly helped themselves to Momma's house. They move in before the dirt settles on the casket.

I am in limbo, spiritually and physically. When everyone leaves, I am finally alone, left in my own thoughts and grief. The sun is creeping in through the tinfoil window above the kitchen sink. It relieves my feeling of darkness.

Dixie slams through the front door, attached to a tall Hispanic man who has more grease in his hair than my morning eggs and bacon. His jet-black mane is slicked back and forms a dandruff side part to the base of his skull. He is wearing a good, old-fashioned wifebeater with his left arm showcasing a tattoo of Jesus Christ him-fucking-self, thorns around the brow, drops of atonement blood, and all that jazz.

Dixie smells of deliriously bad decisions—Mr. Wild Turkey in the flesh with a hint of someone who has completely given up on life and has decided to not shower until the luck turns.

"Heeeeeeyyyyyyyy, Ruby," she says, clearly attempting to pronounce her words in a full effort to not appear seriously fucked up.

In honesty, it is quite an impressive feat.

"Hey," I reply as I ignore them both.

"Or maybe you should say hooooolllllaaaa."

Dixie swings her arms around Mr. Mexico's head and breaks into a fit of giggles.

"Hola! That's Mexican talk for *hello*."

"Where do I put her?" Mr. Mexico politely asks as if he is delivering used furniture from the local Wood and Stool. I can clearly see that he is as anxious to get rid of her as I am as anxious to receive her. Mr. Mexico and I have something in common. It is better to give than to receive.

I motion toward the hallway and give him an affirmative permission slip to carry her to bed.

He promptly returns and says, "See ya."

And then he is gone.

I wait. I stall. I stumble. I crawl. This kind of silence feels dangerous. Dixie usually continues her shenanigans long after visitors leave. But there is no sound coming from her room.

I suppose I could use some of her shenanigans right at this moment. I make my way to the bedroom. I slowly peek inside. I keep in mind that the last few times I peeked in on Dixie, it involved a dead man next to the mustard and her pussy attached to my girlfriend's tongue. I have earned the right to be guarded.

She is lying peacefully on the bed. Her hair traipses over the pillow, and she has a faint smile spilling across her lips. She is so fucking beautiful when she smiles. It feels good to see her smile, because I can't.

She's finally asleep. I wonder if this is what it feels like to be a momma—relief when they finally fall asleep. If truth be told once again, some of Dixie's most shining and glorious moments are when

WEEDS THROUGH THE FLOORBOARDS

she is passed completely out. She is good and safe when she is completely on full-blown shut-the-fuck-up status.

I reach down to kiss her. The child part of me wishes to tuck her in and read her a bedtime story—not the Kingdom kind of bedtime story, where we all burn alive and live in a lake of fire for eternity if we don't say our prayers of "Now I lay me down to fucking sleep, I pray the Lord my soul to keep. If I should die before I wake, I thank thee for this lovely fate." I prefer the kind of bedtime story where we all live in a castle in a beautiful meadow, and it turns out we live dysfunctionally ever after.

I affectionately reach down to pull her covers over her. Then I see it, her arm. Her arm is ever so slightly protruding from under a sheet. It is attached to a needle.

"Oh, shit, Dixie."

All the Kingdom's horses and all the Kingdom's men could not put Dixie Anne Thomas back together again.

*****

Blip. Blip. Blip. Blip. The faded, luminescent jade-green pattern of the machine is predictable and makes me feel safe. Its steady, rhythmic hums embrace me with comfort—the comfort that comes with knowing that Dixie is alive.

The mechanical sound of Dixie hanging on by a thread resonates through the hospital room. The consequences of Dixie hanging on by a thread resonate through my brain.

Her hospital room carries an overwhelming smell of alcohol pads, unknown sterile solutions, and a desperate need to be submerged in these cleansing smells and be scrubbed from my sins. If you stop for one moment and listen closely during the hours of silence, you can hear the last breaths from last lives that were taken in this very cold room.

There is a feeling of death, and I feel fear. I cannot tell if it is their fear of leaving this earth or the fear of staying here. "Do not fear, for I am with you." What a crock.

On day six after Dixie's Unfortunate Arm Candy Incident, she is finally released back into the real world, except this world is not prepared. This turn of events is most fortunate. What is most unfortunate is that Dixie is released into the protective custody of Uncle Kevin.

She slides quietly into the car that Uncle Kevin has thoughtfully parked directly in front of the emergency room entrance of St. Mary's Hospital. Although I would like to believe that he truly cares and is concerned for Dixie, my well-deserved Detroit street cred half envisions him slamming his body to the ground and demanding Vicodin and neck brace number my-trunk-is-full.

Dixie says absolutely nothing as she shares the back seat with me. We all chart our course back to Momma's house. Momma is gone, but even in death, she unites the four of us all in some strange way.

Arm Candy Dixie, Fuck-Face Francis, Shovelin' Kevin, and Insane Ruby Jane—what could possibly go wrong? I am so glad you asked.

PART 2

Chapter 1

THE GREAT DIVIDE

The Fabulous Four quietly settles into Momma's house with the fortunate luck of Momma's last will and testament and Uncle Kevin's remarkable ability to change and rearrange any actual events in the event it will serve him better. Uncle Kevin could rearrange the birth date of Jesus Christ and the intricate menu options of the Last Supper if need be. Give him the date? He will rearrange that shit. All he needs is a reliable typewriter with a no-holds-barred correction ribbon. It is pure genius.

Uncle Kevin immediately joins the Kingdom congregation and is lovingly accepted by Brother Eddie as our Lords of Christ liaison to missionaries in other countries. Uncle Kevin's countless evangelical escapades all over the world have earned him every job he has ever been given. Basically, Jesus pays the bills.

Francis spends her days leading the Bible study of Revelations with the Ladies of Zion at the Fellowship Hall. She performs on cue with perfection like she is famous, as the other ladies adore new blood.

Francis entertains them with endless stories of their archeological digs in Israel, their excavation of the Ark of the Covenant, and their ministries of love and hope with the homeless and the less privileged. The Ladies of Zion all flock to Francis like lost little sheep. It is as if she is the Virgin Mary herself. I believe this could possibly be true on some days.

Uncle Kevin and Aunt Francis have never had kids. They were once pregnant for thirty-eight months, but who am I to judge? I am beginning to believe that the only thing that has come out of her actual vagina is cobwebs and the Dead Sea scrolls.

At home, Dixie still has yet to speak. Since she was discharged from the psycho ward, she lies motionless in my old bed, sleeping for countless hours and refusing to bathe. She does not eat no matter what I offer. She will not talk to me no matter what I say, and she stares at the wall for hours on end.

A part of me believes it might have been better if the needle had been successful in rescuing her from this hell on earth. I am unsure if this is because we are living in the devil's Disneyland or if she is learning to live without the drugs and the alcohol and all things wonderful. Sobriety is a bitch.

It is early on a Monday morning as I hover mindlessly over the irritatingly hot kitchen stove, cracking small white eggs one by one into the pan. I admire how eggshells unseeingly crack wide open, breaking and releasing their feelings. Sometimes, the yokes drift together like long-lost friends or natural partners in crime. At other times, the yolks separate themselves from one another and make every effort to not touch. I understand. I no longer like being touched.

I serve Dixie a small plate of scrambled eggs at the breakfast table. This is my new morning commandment from the God Squad—thou shalt cook and clean and all the in between.

Dixie takes her hand and pushes the food away, as she does most mornings. She continues her stare into nothingness. I need her to speak, to talk to me, one word, any word. Her silence is obnoxiously loud.

"Dixie," I softly plead, "please, Dixie, I need you. You just gotta eat. You cannot go on like this much longer. Just one bite."

WEEDS THROUGH THE FLOORBOARDS

I place the eggs on the fork and gently lift it to her mouth, but I am interrupted.

"What on this blessed earth, Ruby Jane?"

Fuck-Face Francis looks into the unfinished pan of eggs on the stove as she begins to interrogate me.

"I've told you how many times? You don't ever listen, child. No wonder your momma was so disappointed in you. You don't mix the salt with the pepper. Not ever. You salt a part of the eggs. You divide. You pepper a part. You divide. You never mix them together. How many times do I have to tell you this? You must divide!"

A mental image of Moses standing next to me and dividing the scrambled eggs like the Red Egg Sea pops into my brain. This is how crazy I am at this moment.

"I'm sorry," I respond, because I really am sorry that I cannot bounce across the fucking table and physically choke her last breath from her throat.

"Colors don't mix, Ruby, and the sooner you come to accept that, the better life you will have. Colors of no kind, most certainly not black and white. We do exist here together, but we must exist separately. The law of God says it. I say it. Now do it!"

This is my Neapolitan ice cream moment.

"What about sucking off oil boy dicks in random gas station parking lots for money and giving..."

Before I can complete my sentence and with no warning, her fist pummels the back of my skull with full force. My head spins, and my vision doubles. I fall to one knee and support my body with my hand against the stove. She grabs the skillet of eggs from the stovetop and hurls them all over the kitchen floor. She then grasps my hair into her hands and forcefully pulls me to her.

"You better learn your place right here and now, you ungrateful bitch," she commands in my ear. "You think you are better than me? You have a lot to learn. And as God as my witness, if you ever disrespect me like this again, I will personally bury you next to your sorry-ass mother!"

She slowly walks from the kitchen and leaves me to regain my senses.

I move around the kitchen floor on my hands and knees, scooping up the racist scrambled eggs into the palms of my hands. It reminds me of being on the floor of the gas station, crawling around in filth and trying to escape the inevitable. Life.

When the cheap linoleum is finally clean of egg debris, I remain seated on the floor, lean my back against the stove, release a long breath, and feel the rage escape from my eyes in the form of tears and sobs. I am unwanted. I belong on a floor with all the other trash.

The final morning sun is creeping through the small gap in the kitchen curtain. I contemplate my next move like a chess game.

Scenario 1: Swallowing handfuls of All Things Blue with half a bottle of expensive scotch and a nice fuck-you note to the nobodies who don't care.

Scenario 2: Perhaps I could take New Lisa Upton–inspired Howard Johnson's weights and tie them neatly around my waist as I wade into the local community swimming pool, where I've never been because the Kingdom does not allow. I kind of like this option. It feels peaceful and calms me.

Scenario 3: Or how about this? Breathing in exhaust fumes that effortlessly and finally silence me as they gracefully dance into the garage that I don't have.

I can't even plan my own demise right.

And in this small silence where I choose to marinate my bad luck and feel sorry for myself, I cry, and I shout out into the universe, "I fucking hate her! Ah!"

The tears come and don't stop. There is no holding back at this point. It feels therapeutic to release all the anger and the despair. I cannot recall a time that I have cried this hard.

And as the sobs begin to cease and I sit by myself, contemplating my own end and ultimate escape from this wretched earth, I hear a voice say, "You know, if you had half a fucking brain in you, you would start fucking that Negro boy again. That would really giddy up her goat. Or we could kill her in her sleep and bury her sorry ass next to Bobby Ray. There's plenty of room."

This is followed by the most devious laughter I've ever heard in my entire life. And just like that, Dixie Anne Thomas is raised from the dead, just like Lazarus.

*****

The Fabulous Four, and what a sight we are. We have cautiously but successfully learned how to exist together, how to tell elaborate lies together, how to hustle others together, how to use one another to stay alive, and how to fuck up anyone who stands in our way. But it is on one particular day that I know for sure that all the wheels on all the trailers have blasted off like no other.

It is a Monday. Dixie and I return home from our weekly grocery shopping. I am still in charge of all meals, including the racist eggs, per the God Squad. And today, we have landed bountiful bargains thanks to Dixie's faithful commitment to her green stamp collection and her even more generous donation of food stamps for Christ.

Francis sits calmly at the kitchen table, reading her weekly Jesus shit and sipping coffee that we all know has a minimum of three shots of Jim Beam. She fools no one, especially me. I hate her.

As I begin removing the items from the bags, I hear a distinctive sound. Perhaps a whimper? Muffled voices from another room? Is that a small child? Or perhaps a puppy? The thought of a small, furry puppy fills me with joy. I've always wanted a dog, but Daddy never let me have one on account of animals being only here on this earth to eat, not to feed.

I look to Dixie, who has zero reaction, which makes me feel like there is no need to question this most peculiar, unidentifiable noise. And let's be real here. With this group of the Fabulous Four? Questions are utterly dangerous and can only add to the burden of more secrets.

I open the pantry to put away the Toasted Oats, only to see Brother Eddie cowering in the far corner. He is wearing white boxer shorts, a white undershirt, black knee socks, and a really nice pair of patent leather dress shoes. His hands and feet are unfortunately tied together, and his mouth is shoved full of hosiery from Momma's old collection, I assume.

Dixie looks at me, shrugs her shoulders, and says, "Now that's a damned shame, ruining a nice pair of stockings like that."

"What the actual fuck!" I turn to scream at Francis.

"Did you remember the eggs, Ruby Jane?" Francis questions. "Y'all know I have to have my morning eggs. And I have a nice cup of coffee right over there for you, cooling off just the way you like it."

I stand with my mouth open and make efforts to bring myself to speak. The look on my face is clearly and unmistakably communicating the looming concern that is on the floor in the pantry.

Francis then nonchalantly adds, "Oh, one more thing. Eddie here?"

She nods her head toward the far corner of the pantry.

"Don't you pay him no mind. No mind at all. Why, he is just simply a part of God's beautiful plan. We all play a very important part in God's plan."

"What the fuck is wrong with you, Francis? What beautiful plan? He is in our pantry. Not visiting the pantry. He is tied up and IN the pantry. What can you possibly be thinking? W-what is he doing here?"

"Calm down, calm down. You are always so theatrical. No sense in getting your nerves all riled up. Now I may not have all the answers right this second. There are some things I don't know. But what I do know? I do know that if Brother Eddie here is not there to run the ministry and control the Kingdom, well, then your Uncle Kevin most certainly can."

I look at Bother Eddie as his eyes plead with me for help.

"Well, he sure looks like a fag, if you ask me," Dixie interjects.

"Oh my god...what...what is happening...what is actually happening right now? Are you all listening to yourselves right now?" I urgently plead in my last effort to fix something that clearly cannot be repaired.

"How many times do I have to tell you? Don't be so fucking dramatic, Ruby Jane."

WEEDS THROUGH THE FLOORBOARDS

Francis gets up from the table, walks over to me, and places her hands squarely on my shoulders. She stares straight into my eyes.

"Now you better listen up right now. You just never know what good can come from those of us with Christ intentions. Never underestimate your Uncle Kevin, Ruby, not ever. He is not only a great leader, but he is the chosen one—chosen by God for his greatness. And right now, your Uncle Kevin is leading our family to victory in Jesus. And right now? At this very moment? I do know that Brother Eddie is right where he needs to be."

"Right where he needs to be? Have you lost your mind? He is in our food pantry, Francis, with the Cheese Nips! Did you even think this through? Like, did you consider what happens when you let him go? Did you even take one moment to think about this insane plan of yours that you somehow thought would make everything better?"

"Oh, right. Well, since you brought it up, clearly, we can't let him go, you silly girl," Francis adds.

"That's the first thing you've said that makes sense. No shit you can't let him go. What on earth were you thinking?"

"I know a guy—" Dixie starts to add.

"Shut up, Dixie!" I scream. "I don't want any part of this... this...whatever this mess is. Leave me out of it! This never happened. You hear me? Francis, you created this fucking fiasco, and you and you alone can figure out how to get rid of it! I am leaving, and when I get back, this shit better be cleaned up. All of it!"

I slam the door as I leave.

And that is how poor Brother Eddie drowned in an unfortunate swimming incident at the creek next to old man Miller's barn and how Uncle Kevin landed the job of Top God in Charge.

*****

We gather on a Tuesday in honor of Brother Eddie and his commitment and his loyalty to the Pine Creek Pentecostal calling. Fuck-Face Francis plays the organ like the opening of a sold-out Broadway show. I am not sure if she has been hiding her musical talent or hiding her talent to hide secrets.

Uncle Kevin stands in all his glory at the front of the sanctuary, wearing his shiny new black marrying/burying suit he bought at the local Woolworths. He has pinned a tiny white rose on the left lapel and holds his Bible high into the sky as he commands Brother Eddie's soul to join the Kingdom and to sit at the throne next to Jesus's feet.

As Uncle Kevin raises his arm high above his head, I glance down to the ground to notice he is wearing black socks and Brother Eddie's patent leather shoes. A chill runs through my entire body and down my spine.

Uncle Kevin's words flow from his mouth and into the hearts of those grieving. Even I almost believe him. Francis cries on command. We cry on command. The congregation cries on command. And it is at this moment that the God Squad understands that tears make fears, and fears make money, and with this knowledge, we are about to earn what is rightfully ours.

Chapter 2

CAMPFIRE CONFESSIONS

rip. Drip. Drip. Drip.
I lazily lean my body over the kitchen tap, only to realize I am also leaning into a world of complete uncertainty. I have no parents. I have no true home. I have no love to give or receive.

The tap water slowly and casually drips into the tiny glass jars Aunt Dixie and I have ordered from the Sears catalog kitchenware edition. The Israel Jesus Jars are carefully and affectionately filled to the fire and brimstone with holy water brought to the United States from the river Jordan.

The living water has been blessed by Uncle Kevin and currently fetches five whole dollars for one jar. For that amount of money, Jesus should be willing to change that shit into wine or Boone's Farm Strawberry Hill. That would be even better.

In all actuality, Dixie and I fill the jars from the cold agnostic tap water at the kitchen sink while we playfully sip MD 20/20 and smoke an enormous amount of weed and watch *The Price Is Right*. I love that show.

It is a Thursday. What seems like a perfectly fucked-up day is about to prove that there is actually a day well beyond that connotation. Words are powerful.

Dixie and I have finally completed our very last jar of an enormous Holy, Holy, Holy Lord God Almighty order when Uncle Kevin calmly walks into the kitchen. Uncle Kevin has been most vigilant to his God Squad calling since the Pantry Pandemonium Incident.

"We…we…well, how do I say this? We have a…well…we have a problem," he firmly states as he painfully sits down at the kitchen table.

Dixie and I instantly freeze and silently glance at each other in collective fear. We have never known Uncle Kevin to use the word *problem* to describe any of our past unfortunate situations, which makes us terrified of what is coming next.

"What is going on?" Dixie asks anxiously.

Uncle Kevin doesn't respond. He remains seated, and his face shows me that I need to perhaps be concerned.

"Kevin, look at me. Tell me, what is going on?" Dixie pleads. "Hey, look at me. I am here."

She gently touches her hand to his face to direct his glaze to hers. I imagine that this intimate and private conversation has already occurred at some point in their past, perhaps when they were children.

Dixie then affectionately reaches for his hand and holds it lovingly inside hers as if predicting the protection Kevin is not only about to need but will also most certainly need later.

Uncle Kevin stares back as if he is trying to put his words of wisdom and explanation together.

"There has been…well, there has been an accident," Kevin finally says.

"What kind of accident? Kevin, what the fuck is going on?" Dixie demands. "You are freaking me out! Just say it!"

"Okay, okay. Dixie, stop screaming. You know I don't like the screaming."

He grabs his ears with his hands to mute the noise.

Suddenly, the phone rings. We all stop in silence and stare at one another, our eyes wide with fear and our imaginations even wider with possible, impending mayhem.

"Don't answer that!" Kevin demands.

Dixie jumps up from her chair and grabs the receiver, forcing it to her ear.

"Hello? Yes, this is Dixie. What? Are you sure? Yes, of course, I understand. This is just simply terrible. Yes, again, I understand. I will make sure that Brother Kevin knows, and we will help in any way we can. Just let us know what you all need. Oh, and thank you for calling. God bless you."

I may or may not need to vomit.

Dixie hangs up the phone and looks at Uncle Kevin as a sheepish grin covers her face.

"You little devil, you."

She laughs as she playfully punches Kevin repeatedly in the shoulder.

"You fucking genius!"

"What? What is this all about?"

I am officially becoming impatient. Am I crazy? Am I literally asking to be a part of another secret?

Dixie continues.

"A problem? How is this a problem, Kev? How? This is brilliant. Oh, sorry, Ruby Jane. So it appears that your clever Uncle Kevin had an unexpected fire at the church, and I am guessing we will now collect the insurance money. Right, Kevin? Church burns. Insurance forged. We collect the money. Story over."

Dixie leans her head back and laughs at her impending potential of fortune.

"Uncle Kevin?" I ask. "Is this true?"

"Well, it's kind of true…kind of," he responds reluctantly.

"Kind of? What the fuck kind of answer is that? Did you burn down the church? Like, I am not judging you. Well, not yet," I add. "If we collect the insurance money and the police don't get involved, I can see your point. This ain't my first church-burning extravaganza."

I slide my eyes to Dixie.

"Yeehaw! Why, just think of all the possibilities that are about to land in our laps. We can rebuild and rebuild bigger and better. Oh, and we can…we can get a loan! Oh, Kev, we can get an actual loan from the bank and have access to all that money! This is so good right now."

Dixie is dancing around the kitchen. Uncle Kevin, however, is sitting motionless, staring off into space, and clearly has not bought into our church-burning cheerleading antics.

"So what is the fucking problem?" Dixie finally asks. "How on earth is this a problem? Church burns. Kevin is the God boss. We have access to all the money. Everyone trusts Kevin. How is this possibly a problem?"

Kevin eventually exhales a long, extended sigh and begins to forcefully massage his temples with his long fingers before he finally speaks.

"Francis was inside," he says in despair.

"Francis was inside where?" Dixie asks.

The air leaves the room. There is nothing but silence. Secrets.

"What do you mean…inside?" I respond, feeling completely panicked. "Did you know she was there when…did you… Fuck! What are you saying right now?"

The uncomfortable silence is finally broken by Dixie, who says, "Well, that is for sure a damn shame, Kevin. I am really sorry."

"Thank you, Dixie. I really appreciate that."

Dixie smiles and politely adds, "Just to be perfectly clear, I am sorry that you actually wasted a match on that bitch."

And then there were three.

*****

The three of us sit anxiously in a small, cold room that contains nothing more than a metal table and a pitch-black telephone that has a cord resembling the curlicue fries at the Burger Barn. I feel like I am in the middle of a *Hill Street Blues* episode as we rehearse line after line of possible outcomes as we are questioned by the police.

WEEDS THROUGH THE FLOORBOARDS

And while I am overwhelmingly nervous and physically sick to my stomach, Dixie has her head flat against the cold table, and the obvious appears: Dixie feels right at home.

"Hello. I am sorry to keep you waiting."

A tall, handsome man enters the room and takes a seat at the end of the table.

"Hey there, Dixie."

He shyly looks her way. The look on his face tells me immediately that these two have been entangled in some sort of shady-as-shit past.

"Hey there, Roy. I am good. It's good to see you. How is Marcie?"

"She's good. She's good," Officer Roy replies.

He clears his throat, takes out a mini spiral notepad from his pocket that has surely seen better days, and pretends to look busy as he writes eagerly onto the miniscule pages.

"So can I ask you? Would there be any reason why Ms. Francis was at the church in the middle of the night? I am just asking because...well...it just seems a bit, well, it just seems odd. Why would someone be in a church in the middle of the night?"

Uncle Kevin is swift and the first to answer.

"It may seem out of character to a heathen such as yourself, but our God, the God we serve, is open twenty-four hours a day, seven days a week. Perhaps if you knew Christ as your personal Savior, you wouldn't find it out of character for his disciples to be worshipping him at all hours of the day and night. God doesn't sleep!"

Officer Roy stares at Uncle Kevin as if attempting to manipulate him into the continuation of a possible confessional conversation.

"What I don't understand," Officer Roy says, "it is just unusual for—"

"Goddamn it, Roy!" Dixie interjects. "For fuck's sake, we are all adults here. Just say what you wanna say so we can get the fuck out of here. I have shit to do."

Officer Roy shoots Dixie a warning glance and reaches back down to his notebook to jot something down that appears very important.

145

Uncle Kevin takes a deep breath and offers a truce to this uncomfortable situation.

"Look, Officer Roy, is it? Okay, Roy. I don't know what you are implying, but I can tell you that I only learned of Francis being inside of the church when the Yell County Fire Department came to put it out. And no, it was not uncommon for Francis to go to the church at all hours. It is a part of our job.

"I have no idea how the fire started, and I surely cannot provide you with exact reasons as to why Francis was there today. Other than that, I don't know what additional information I could possibly provide. Now if you will kindly excuse us, we have other matters to attend to."

Uncle Kevin stands, and following his lead, we make our way to the door.

"Bye, Roy. Tell Marcie I said I hate her," Dixie spits the words over her shoulder as I push her to the door.

"Wait, wait. Please," Officer Roy pleads. "I just have one more question, and then I will let you go. I know you are busy and have other things to attend to, but if you could just give me one more minute of your time. Please."

"What is it?" Uncle Kevin impatiently demands.

"So if Ms. Francis was night-worshipping Christ at three in the morning, as you claim to be the case, can you then offer a reason as to why she left a note?"

Officer Roy slowly slides a white piece of paper across the table. I look to Uncle Kevin for some sort of instruction, but he offers none.

"She left a note under the wiper of her car in the church parking lot."

He takes the note and pushes it toward us. Uncle Kevin reaches down, and as he unfolds the paper, the three of us guardedly lean over in anticipation of our next secret. It simply reads, "It is well with my soul."

"She was found lying across the prayer altar, Mr. Kevin. Can you offer any insight as to her state of mind the past month? Was she depressed? Did she say anything to anyone that might help us understand where her head was? Why would she set fire to a church and choose to lie over an altar? We all find this very unnerving. Bottom line, we believe Ms. Francis set the fire intentionally."

Kevin dramatically grabs the note and clutches it to his chest. Tears flood from his eyes as he places the back of his hand over his mouth in an attempt to muffle his cries.

"Absolutely not! I don't believe you! My sweet Francis would never do such a thing. Why would she do such a thing intentionally? Why?"

Uncle Kevin then drops to his knees and begins sobbing uncontrollably. Dixie and I rush down to him to comfort him. I place my arms around him and squeeze him tight.

"It's okay, Uncle Kevin. We will handle this. As a family, we will deal with this. I am just so sorry."

I sob along with Aunt Dixie. At this point, Officer Roy is grabbing for tissues not only for us but also for himself. Our performances are simply brilliant.

Officer Roy walks over to Uncle Kevin and places his hand on his shoulder.

"I am so very sorry for your loss, Mr. Kevin."

He continues to wipe tears from his eyes.

"It's Brother Kevin. And thank you very much. Can we leave now?"

Officer Roy scrambles to help Uncle Kevin up from his knees and to the door.

"Of course, of course. Thank you for your time. I will close the investigation today, and if you need anything, anything at all, the Yell County Police Department is here to help you in any way we can."

"Thank you," Uncle Kevin barely responds. "That means the world to us."

We walk out of the police station, the three of us, scattering trails of secrets behind us. We pile into the car, and all three of us are gathered in total silence.

Uncle Kevin stares ahead and turns the ignition, but the car stays in place.

"Well, that went well," he finally says with a smile of relief on his face.

"The fuck it did, Kevin," Dixie spouts off. "Seriously, what were you thinking? Do you know how bad this could have gone? Do you only think of yourself? Next time you up and decide to kill your wife, you might wanna fucking let me know, you asshole. You put us all at risk!"

"Are you seriously saying that to me right now? What gives you the right to say this to me? Might I remind you of a certain refrigerator incident in which I came and assisted with no complaints whatsoever?"

Uncle Kevin is becoming angry at this point, an emotion I have yet to see.

"I didn't kill my wife, Dixie Anne, and don't you ever say that again! I will not sit here and tolerate that kind of blaspheme. I loved Francis with everything in me, and I did not kill her!"

"You are telling me that the church burned, you knew about it, and Francis was accidentally inside and just by chance left a note on her windshield? You have lost your ever-loving mind if you think for one minute I believe that! Just admit it, Kevin!"

Dixie is screaming at this point.

"Calm down. Everyone, please just calm down," I request as I try to ease the tension due to the fact that we are still in the parking lot of the police station. "Let's just take a breath and talk about what happened. There is no need to be angry. We only have each other, and we need to be supportive."

"You are right, Ruby Jane," Dixie agrees. "I am sorry, Kev. I just…I just don't understand. I am sorry I accused you of killing your beloved wife in a fire and laying her over the altar—"

"And I am sorry I reminded you that you killed your fiancé and stuffed him into a fridge for me to take care of!" Kevin mocks back in the voice of a five-year-old.

"STOP IT! NOW! Both of you, stop this. I killed a dude at the truck stop. Okay? Do you hear me? I did it! Are we all even now? Can we just fucking leave this parking lot and go home?" I shout.

They both come to a complete standstill and turn to stare at me, as I am seated in the back seat, with their eyes chock-full of shock.

"What? What the fuck are you looking at? So y'all are the only ones allowed to kill people? How sanctimonious is that?"

"Well, no, I am not saying that," Uncle Kevin contributes. "It's just that—okay, I appreciate your honesty. Well, since you are being honest, I suppose I will be too. I didn't kill Francis. Well, not personally. But I may or may not know a guy who perhaps—"

"Oh, for Jesus's sake, Kev," Dixie implodes. "You are so fucking obnoxious. Just because you didn't light the match doesn't mean you didn't kill her!"

"I didn't kill her. I simply served in the leadership capacity to an assistant who encountered an unfortunate series of events that aligned to needed and necessary measures that simply could not be overlooked."

"You fucking killed her!"

Dixie is fiercely adamant.

"And I dare you to say you didn't, you almighty liar!"

"Well, we have $250,000 in life insurance coming to us that says I did nothing of the sort," Kevin retorts.

There is nothing but speechlessness as Uncle Kevin slowly and finally pulls the car from the parking lot of the police station, where we have spent way too much time debating *Murder, She Wrote*.

The silence is finally broken when Dixie takes a calming breath and says, "It is such a relief to know that not only was I completely wrong about you, Kevin. I apologize for my blatant accusations that are clearly unsubstantiated and unwarranted."

Uncle Kevin smiles, warmly delighted. There is officially a peaceful financial understanding among us as we drive home.

Uncle Kevin parks the car in the driveway. We sit together, contemplating the ending to a most emotional day.

He calmly turns to me and says, "Ruby Jane, honey, I do owe you a heartfelt apology. I am so sorry that I did not even pay notice to your words earlier. It was, quite frankly, rude and disrespectful, and I want to personally apologize for my blatant disregard of your feelings. I should always be attentive to your confessions and feelings, and for that, I ask your understanding and forgiveness."

"Of course, Uncle Kevin. I just found myself in a terrible situation, and things got out of hand, and—"

Uncle Kevin cuts me off midsentence.

"There, there. It is done. No more need to talk about it. The one thing that you need to learn as you encounter this earthly experience is that talking out loud about unplanned and unfortunate circumstances only delivers unresolved dangers and problems into your existence. You know how you solve problems?"

I truly contemplate this question.

"Prayer?" I innocently answer.

"Oh, heavens, no, you sweet child."

He is bellowing into a deep belly laugh.

When he gains his composure, he adds, "You don't talk. You never talk, Ruby Jane, not ever. If you decide it is absolutely necessary to run your mouth and to talk? You only talk about solutions. Solutions are not only the answer. They are also the resolution in all circumstances. Now do you need a shovel?"

Chapter 3

OL' ROY

Several months pass, and life meticulously begins to return to some sort of normal. As the Pine Creek Pentecostal Church is being repaired from the Francis Flames Incident, we now congregate in the Fellowship Hall for all our weekly services.

Not only are we structurally rebuilding, but we are also building our membership. More members mean more money, and more money means more happiness. Anyone who has ever said money can't buy you happiness just has never had any money.

I am quickly learning that there is an obnoxious amount of money to be made in the Jesus industry, and we are making it. We are paid for all things Christ, which makes me feel better about not going to school. Who needs high school when I can pour tap water into jars and pocket five hundred bucks?

Don't get me wrong. This is a hard job. I bust my ass all day every day, hustling for Jehovah. Come up with an idea? The lost sheep will follow. All it takes is faith—faith that these morons believe anything you tell them.

Holy water? Sold. Drive-through prayers on Thursdays with an offering plate? Sold. Orphans in Africa who need saving? Sold. Sister Francis Memorial Fund? Sold. Gay conversion therapy? Sold.

The money flows like the river Jordan. We want for nothing, including the best drugs Jesus money can buy. Dixie has set us up for tremendous success in the drug extravaganza. We have connections that would make the Mexican cartel jealous.

On this particular day, the cartel sure could come in handy. It is a Friday. I am filling Mason jars with Jesus water when the phone rings.

"Ruby, I need you."

Dixie sounds panicked.

"What's wrong? Where are you? Are you okay?"

"Ruby, honey, I need you to really listen to me. Are you listening?"

"Yes. What is it? Dixie, you are scaring me."

"I need you to come to me. I need you to stay calm and follow my directions. Can you do that for me, honey?"

"Yes. What is going on? What do you need me to do?"

"Ruby, I need you to come to me. I am at the Ramada Inn Motel on Lake Drive, room 143. Make sure no one sees you. Can you do that for me, honey?"

I immediately slam the phone down, grab the keys to Uncle Kevin's van, and drive as fast as I can, all while trying to assess what I am up against. I decide to cautiously park behind the dumpster at the Quick Mart directly across the street from the Ramada Inn.

When I locate room 143, I conduct FBI-worthy surveillance, and then I knock. Dixie slowly opens the door.

"Are you alone?"

"No, bitch. I brought Moses and the Wise Men! Of course, I am alone. Let me in before someone sees us."

Dixie reaches out, grabs my arm, and pulls me into the motel room.

"Dixie, what is going on?" I plead, as she sits on the bed and buries her face in her hands.

WEEDS THROUGH THE FLOORBOARDS

Dixie begins sobbing uncontrollably, and I am at a loss. Her tears are pouring from her eyes. She looks like she has been up for days, but a foul smell impedes my nostrils, which makes me believe it may have been longer.

I crouch in front of her, sit on the floor to face her, and calmly grasp her hands and squeeze them tight. I afford her this rare moment to release her feelings while I patiently wait. Dixie deserves patience.

However, this does not afford her the end to her flow of tears. What Dixie may not know is that when she hurts, I hurt more. When she aches, I ache more. I only want to make her better.

As floods of tears cover her face, I race into the bathroom to find tissues. But unfortunately, before I have the ability to discover tissues, I discover Officer Roy on the bathroom floor. He is lying on his back. He has a tiny, thin white line traipsing underneath his nose, and his eyes are wide open. He is clearly not breathing.

"Dixie! What the fuck!"

"I know, I know, I know. I am sorry. I can explain," she says.

"There ain't time to explain," I shout from the bathroom.

My Clancy gangster instincts kick into full force, and I am now the leader of this family.

"Okay, okay. It is okay. Take a breath. Did anyone see him come in with you?" I ask as Dixie sits, rocking back and forth on the bed.

"Of course not. He always parks at the Visitor Tourist Center, and I pick him up. This is his room. He rents it for us to…well…"

"Did anyone see you?"

"No, I don't think so. I, well, I have only stayed here a few times. We usually stay at Lakeside Inn, but they had a coupon for tonight, and I—"

"Stop! I don't fucking care about a coupon, Dixie. We have a dead cop, a married dead cop, in a motel room with a massive amount of drugs."

This is the part where the cartel sure could have helped.

I reach down in front of Dixie at the foot of the bed, grab her shoulders, and say, "Dixie, here, take the keys to the van and leave. Go home. I will handle this. Cross the street. It is behind the dumpster. Now go."

"I cannot leave you with this…with this mess."

"Yes, yes, you can. Dixie, I need you to listen to me. I need you to go home. Take the van and go straight home. Hand me your keys, Dixie. I will take care of everything."

Dixie inhales a deep breath, grabs me, and squeezes out the life that is left in me.

"I love you, Ruby Jane."

"I love you more. Now get the fuck out of here."

I sit on the bed. I contemplate my game plan. I am a Clancy, and it is my time to shine. I proceed to wipe down every item in the motel. I would like to confess that I don't finish off all the coke in the bathroom, but that would be a straight-up lie. I snort that shit from left to right, then right to left. And since this story is all about truth, Officer Roy was a fucking wimp if this shit killed him.

I remove all signs of Dixie Anne from the room and rearrange it so that it will deliver an unquestionable story, including the strategic positioning of the hardcover lime-green Gideon's Bible, which I stage to the left of ol' Roy's body.

Officer Roy will be found in a most unfortunate incident of recreational drug usage that sadly has proven to be lethal. They will find him lying on the intricate red-and-silver polyester bedcover with the television on *Wheel of Fortune* and the Bible opened to the book of Psalms.

"Yea, though I snort through the valley of the shadow of death, thy coke and thy Jim Beam, they comfort me."

Before I make my flawless exit from the scene of the crime that didn't happen, I actually remove all the cash from his wallet and take his wedding ring. And for ol' Roy's sake, I take his gun, just in case I don't have a shovel.

Chapter 4

RIFFRAFF

I cautiously make an attempt to open my eyes, which happen to be solidly pasted together like rubber cement glue. I look around me. My head is blazing, and my mouth mimics the lake of fire as I wish for Lazarus to deliver that one drop of water on my tongue.

The brutal early-morning rays of light shine through the dilapidated blinds. I am at Dixie's trailer, a convenient getaway that we escape to when we need a break from the Jesus Broadway show.

Acting like a Christian is a full-time job and an exhausting role to play. There are countless unmanageable rules and regulations that one must uphold at all times while being watched and observed. It is most difficult, to say the very least.

I am currently granted apostolic immunity at the church on account of being blood related to the Top God In Charge. As the fog slowly creeps from my brain and I lie in the silence, I take in a deep breath and fill my lungs with much-needed oxygen. I have learned to appreciate being alone.

It is at this moment that I hear a soft, sultry "Good morning." The unexpected voice jolts me out of my drug- and alcohol-induced coma. I have no memory of last night. I have no memory of the last three days, and for the love of God, I have no idea who this woman is in my bed.

"Oh, hey, good morning," I reply.

Does she know that I do not know who she is? Does she care that I do not know who she is? What have I done?

She gracefully rolls toward me and presses her naked body against my chest as she brushes her hands through my hair. Confession: her touch makes me feel calm and safe.

"Hey, Ruby. Last night was wonderful, the absolute best."

"Yes, it was."

Was it?

"Oh my god, I have never done anything like that! Don't get me wrong, I am not gay or nothin' like that. I just…well…had a really good time. But hey, I hate to fuck and run, but I am late for my shift at the Taco Villa. I gotta bail. Catch ya later?"

Tina! That is her name. Taco Villa equals Tina. I love their hot sauce.

"Sure."

And with that, Taco Villa Tina leaves me alone in my bed, contemplating where I left my panties and my shirt and my keys and my dignity. Dignity is overrated.

I suddenly smell the strong scent of fried bacon seeping through the air. Who the fuck else did I bring home, and why are they cooking in the kitchen? I slowly drag my ass out of bed and stabilize my hungover body with both sides of the trailer walls as I blindly feel my way to the kitchen.

"Well, hey there, baby!" she screams from the kitchen.

Oh no, what have I done?

There she stands, in the flesh. How did this happen? I swore that never ever again would I… She is wearing one of my T-shirts. Her hair is softly cascading down the side of her shoulder. Her emerald-green eyes are magnified in the sunlight. She is absolutely more beautiful than ever.

"Hey, Netti," I say like I am defeated, because if truth be told, I am.

WEEDS THROUGH THE FLOORBOARDS

"Here you go, baby. Take some of this, and you will feel so much better."

She utilizes the bacon spatula to perfectly organize a small line of coke down the side of the kitchen table. She leans over to hand me a straw, just far enough that I can see the tips of her nipples under the oversized T-shirt.

I would like to say I reluctantly give in, but in all honesty, there is no reluctance when it comes to Netti. I snort into my nose so deep and so aggressively I feel the coke mold its way into my veins and into my emotions, numbing both.

Netti lays the bacon in front of me with an additional side of coke, neatly organized and perfectly straight. Hmm, fried bacon with a side of coke. I wonder if that would actually be a profitable item on the Waffle House menu.

"Listen, I gotta run. I got places to be and people to see."

Netti reaches down and softy kisses me on the cheek.

"You have a nice day, Ruby Doobie. And the next time you wanna fuck around in bi-ways, freeways, and three-ways? Tina is our girl. Who knew you had it in you, Ruby!"

I am thinking the exact same thing.

*****

It is Sunday service. I am violently hungover, and my legs shake profusely from being spread like PB&J for the last twelve hours. Netti and Taco Villa Tina are quite frankly making me wish for a most untimely death on certain mornings after hours of recreational lick-and-split. I would not be far-fetched to admit that I surely would qualify for the Olympic version, if only it existed. Olympic Team Ruby!

How am I to perform unmentionable sexual favors to multiple receivers for six hours straight, ingest cocktails of multiple-minded drugs, and be expected to wake up and be cast into the leading role of Jesus lover? It's a fair and reasonable question.

On this particular heaven day, I am effectively cast for the coveted starring role of Smiler-Greeter-Secret-Pussy-Eater to all our diligent and reliable congregation, a role I am most comfortable with. I attempt to manage a chronological timeline that only serves in my favor—drugs, drink, sex, drugs, sex, drink, sex, sex, church. Rinse and repeat.

I have learned that in an organized timeline, it is most efficient to align the eighth hour of planned activities to a resilient bump of the Devil's Snow so that I can maintain a surge of energy required to play Sinner-Greeter to our worship service.

While the beloved parishioners file into place, Dixie organizes the children's service that takes place at the altar in the front of the sanctuary. The God Squad has learned that while there most certainly exists a massive amount of money to be made in the God facade, there is existentially much more money to be made when you place children into the mixture of the God plus parenting equation. That equals money galore.

Parents must be vigilantes to ensure that their birthed spiritual warriors will be with them in the afterlife. Anything short of this is eternal damnation into the lake of never-ending fire. But not to worry. God still loves you. He just wants you to burn to death forever.

I stand at the front glass entrance, handing out the bulletin schedules for the service, and it is at this time that I hear a familiar tune drift to my ears from the grand piano.

> Jesus loves the little children, all the children of
> the world.
> Red and yellow, black and white. They are pre-
> cious in his sight.
> Jesus loves the little children of the world.

I choke back my uncontrollable urge to vomit last night's Wild Turkey all over the floor. Let's be honest. Call a spade a spade. Jesus loves the little children. Jesus just does not love the little gay children, period, end of discussion. Jesus does not love me. He never will. I am not precious in his sight. I sicken him. I am not accepted. I am not loved. I am unwanted.

WEEDS THROUGH THE FLOORBOARDS

I often wonder where God was on Granddaddy Tuesdays and Oil Boy Wednesdays. Once again, it's a fair argument.

My thoughts are suddenly interrupted by a clear commotion resonating from the direction near the piano.

"No, you will not talk to me that way!" screams Dixie from the front of the sanctuary.

"I did no such thing. I simply told the truth," Sister Nancy Shaw sasses back to Dixie.

Allow me to introduce Sister Nancy Shaw. She has three rowdy-as-fuck boys by three rowdy-as-fuck men and smells like potato salad and blue Windex. We all know that her last husband left her high and dry on account of her taking up with Travis Connor in the back parking lot after Saturday youth fellowship.

Dixie raises herself from the steps, where she has been seated with all the unmanageable asshole toddlers from actual hell, and she aggressively approaches Sister Nancy. I suck in and anxiously hold my breath, as I am innately aware of what is possibly about to happen.

A. Dixie throat-punches Sister Nancy Shaw.
B. Dixie effortlessly picks Sister Nancy Shaw up and throws her over the altar.
C. Dixie puts Sister Nancy Shaw in her Bobby Refrigerator.
D. All of the above.

"Thank you, Sister Nancy, for your voiced concerns. I will certainly take your comments into prayerful and thoughtful consideration. If you will excuse me."

Dixie jolts up the aisle, avoiding all eyes at all costs. I quickly follow her into the pastoral office, where I find her lighting up a Virginia Slims, biting her nails to the quick, and pacing from one side of the office to the other.

"Dixie? What is going on? What happened?"

"That cunt! That fucking bitch! She thinks she is better than me? I will fucking kill her in her sleep and—"

"No. Dixie, stop! Stop. Calm down and put that cigarette out, for fuck's sake! You need to remember where we are right now! What happened? I need you to calm down and talk to me."

"That bitch has the nerve to tell me to my face that I am nothing more than white trash and don't belong here, much less put here to mold and lead our children! Can you believe she said that to me, Ruby Jane? Did she really just call me trash?"

Her eyes are brimming with tears. Uh-oh. It looks like our apostolic immunity contract is officially over.

"I am sure she didn't mean what she said, Dixie."

"Yes, she absolutely meant it, and she said the same thing about you! She called you awful names and told me we didn't belong here, neither one of us, and that there was talk that they was gonna vote us out on account of us being wicked and sinful. Do they even know how much we do here?"

The real question is, do they really know what we do here? I am silenced for a moment, and after thoughtful brainstorming with the potential crisis that looms in our future, I respond.

"Oh, really? They said that about me too?"

I contemplate. Now that it is directed at me as well, it somehow feels different and more personal.

"Yes," Dixie continues. "She says that she is going to make it her mission to let all the Ladies of Zion and every congregant know what we really are—trash and sinners."

"That is simply not going to happen, Dixie. Now don't worry. Everything is gonna be okay. You know how she is. Why, Nancy Shaw ain't nothing but a talkaholic, running her mouth to any poor soul within a foot of her. Just calm yourself, and let's get back to the service. I will take care of everything."

I calmly return to the morning service, which is now in full progress. I participate. I act. I respond. I smile. I cry. I do my thing. I play my part. I work very hard, because I truly know that this work will pay off in the end—pay off in the monetary way, not so much in the Jesus-paid-our-debts way.

I allow myself a break so that I can resonate on the possible, potential, impending problem. I also allow ample time to slit all four tires on Sister Nancy Shaw's Chevrolet Impala. If she doesn't behave herself and continues to entertain her current accusations and insults? Rest assured that her tires are not the only thing I will slit.

Chapter 5

FELIZ NAVIDAD

I hate Christmas, and as the imminent birth of our Savior approaches, I find every single reason to avoid the annoying, melodic carols and the never-ending clattering of the Salvation Army bell outside the local Kmart.

And while I do have the utmost respect for the fact that Monty Cartright dresses in a full Santa Claus suit, I have more respect that he does not stammer around and fall over. Because not only is Monty Cartright a superior, constant talent at ringing the bell, he is also a superior, constant talent at secretly sipping his 150-proof eggnog and looking at women's tits. I find no blame in this. I love both—booze and tits.

Dixie and I have spent the last three nights at her trailer, smoking weed, sipping champagne out of fancy red glasses shaped like reindeer, and preparing glittery red, green, and silver paper stars for the Giving Tree at the church.

The general idea of the Giving Tree is an idea of epic proportions. This is a solid business strategy to create the facade that a child or a family is in desperate need of an absolute life essential. The

WEEDS THROUGH THE FLOORBOARDS

heartbreaking need can be as simple as a used winter coat for poor Timmy whose momma has no heat, or an extravagant bike for sweet Sara who needs to help her invalid momma with the grocery shopping so the family doesn't starve.

Whoever the fuck they are, we create their fictitious miserable little lives while we smoke and sip and lounge around a kitchen table in a trailer park. I feel it far more necessary to fundraise for the more fun Christmas essentials, like coke, Jack Daniel's, and regular titty bar escapades.

Don't get me wrong, we don't actually buy the much-needed gifts for the Angels Unaware Project. We just collect the money. Then we spend the money. And nothing will fire up the desire of giving for Christ when you've got a bunch of make-believe orphans in need of a memorable Christmas.

And I am about to experience my own memorable Christmas—not in a "Oh, Holy Night" kinda way, but more like a "Oh, Holy Shit" kinda way.

It is Saturday afternoon. Dixie and I are artistically placing the finishing touches on our Angels Unaware Giving Tree Make-Believe Pretend Project.

Unannounced, Uncle Kevin rushes into the trailer. Uncle Kevin no longer knocks. Dixie and I actually like this. It shows that he trusts us, and we now trust one another. He is wearing a hilarious white beard with a Walmart Santa hat mounted sideways on his head.

Dixie cannot withhold her laughter.

"What on earth, Kev!"

"Well, hello, my sweet, lovely sisters in Christ," he sings pleasantly as his smile flashes from ear to ear.

"What is it now, Uncle Kev?" I reply in a most tragic tone.

His peculiar excitement and pageantry feels most expectant of a future need, which we will be required to fulfill.

Uncle Kevin lets out a ho ho ho and boldly slaps down a stack of scattered papers onto the kitchen table. Dixie does not even look up. She is not impressed.

"What is this?" Dixie asks.

"Well, don't just sit there. Look at it, silly."

Dixie slowly picks up the papers and turns them over. I see a smile come to her lips. She is so beautiful when she smiles.

"What?" Dixie screams and suddenly leaps from the chair to hug Uncle Kevin's neck.

Her legs lock around his waist, and she squeals like a child truly happy on a perfect Christmas morning. I, however, am left in the complete dark.

"Well, Ruby Jane?" Uncle Kevin encourages and awaits an answer.

"I have no idea what is going on right now, but my initial answer is hell to the fuck no. Whatever it is? Pretty sure I'm gonna sit this one out."

"We," Uncle Kevin states as he uses his index finger to point to each of us individually, "we are taking a much-needed vacation!"

Dixie's squeals become louder and louder.

"A vacation! I ain't never been anywhere! Oh, Kevin, this is the best gift ever!"

I, however, can only question the motive behind any vacation that happens to be right in the middle of the most religious and money-making time of any Jesus church on the planet.

Uncle Kevin seems to sense my reluctance.

"Ruby Jane? What do you think? How would you like a little getaway?"

"Where?" I dreadfully respond.

"Mexico!" Dixie screams as she cha-chas through the kitchen.

"Mexico?" I reiterate to ensure I heard correctly.

"Yes, Mexico," Kevin confirms.

I don't have a good feeling about this. It's one thing to fuck up in Yell County. It's quite another thing to fuck up in Mexico.

"Hear me out," Uncle Kevin continues.

"This is very important. We tirelessly and endlessly serve God, and now God will grant us a time to rest. Even God rested on the seventh day when he created the world, and we deserve a seventh-day rest."

"But why are we even thinking about leaving during Christmas?" I question.

My question is ignored. Again, I do not have a good feeling about this.

"Everything is already taken care of. I have all of your travel documents. I have taken care of the airlines and the hotel. The only thing you two gorgeous ladies have to do is pack your bags! We are going to finally relax and receive the gifts that God has graciously bestowed upon us. We leave Monday. I will pick you up at 7:00 a.m. sharp! Don't be late!"

As Uncle Kevin leaves, Dixie continues her Espanola celebrations.

"Can you believe it, Ruby Jane? Us? You and me? Mexico?"

She is sensing my "Bah, humbug!" reluctance and complete lack of enthusiasm.

"Now come on, what's the matter with you? Don't be a Scrooge! This is gonna be amazing. Just you wait and see! Oh, Lord, Ruby Jane, we have so much to do. We gotta get them cute swimsuits and sun hats. Oh, wait. I wanna get one of them fancy straw hats that swallow you up with the grass brim, just like Ginger on *Gilligan's Island*," she continues as I fade into another conversation in my head.

A getaway to Mexico during Cashmas, aka Christmas? Maybe Uncle Kevin is right. We all need a getaway. But while I work to build up excitement for our impending international travels, all that fills my mind is a Holiday Inn Express Getaway.

*****

I spend all of Sunday furiously memorizing the entire map of Mexico. I would like to say that it is to enhance my potential sightseeing knowledge, but if truth be told, it is to make sure I know where the fuck my exit row is in the event that it is in my best interest to flee.

We arrive at the airport on Monday. The putrid smell of wild jet fumes makes me feel nauseated, but my excitement for world adventures has finally taken hold over my fear. The Little Rock airport unfolds in front of me, and I am keen to observe all the possible scenarios with a front-row seat. It is like a movie playing stories that are happening in real time as I watch and wait to board our flight.

I observe butch, manly men hugging and slapping one another on the back and squeezing one another tight. I witness women hugging their children and crying as they are saying hello and goodbye.

I wonder if Momma ever cried after hugging me. Part of me would like to think that she did, but we all know mommas cannot love their lesbian daughters. It is not allowed in the Kingdom. I don't blame her.

As the wheels leave the runway and the jet pulls its way up through the quilted white clouds, I lean against the window and witness the beauty of the earth from above—the radiant blue skies, the jagged mountains, the snake-shaped rivers, and the multicolored patches of land, each connected and quilted to the next like an unplanned jigsaw puzzle needing to be solved.

It is at this moment that I realize I am calmly serene and safeguarded even though I am thousands of feet in the air, because for the first time in my life, I am actually seated on a real-life exit row.

*****

"Can you believe it? Ruby Jane, we are actually here!" Dixie shrieks as we parade ourselves to the entrance of the hotel.

The Mexico air carries unique fragrances that are unknown to Yell County. There is a heavy scent of sweet gardenias followed by a wave of honey and cinnamon. It reminds me of the Sunday French toast Momma used to prepare for me on my birthday. I miss Momma.

We have wanted for nothing since our departure. We have people to drive for us, to carry bags for us, and to smile for no reason.

The hotel room door opens to a magnificent suite that directly overlooks the ocean. Upon entering, Uncle Kevin and Dixie make their way throughout the enormous space and baptize the rooms with their vocal accolades and praises for each adornment that we lack at home.

However, my attention is only directed to the topaz water and white-sand beach that lies in full view in front of my eyes. I mean, I have seen pictures in Momma's old *National Geographic* magazines, but seeing it now in real life is overwhelming and unexpected.

I am roused with all sorts of different emotions, because I have never seen anything this beautiful in my entire life.

I slowly open a door leading to the outside and step out onto a spacious patio. I am surrounded by a plush tropical garden that hovers over my head, and below me, I hear the sound of the waves crashing onto the sand.

The smell of sea salt drifts through my nostrils and unclutters my mind. I watch the waves bubble up onto the shoreline, only to be rejected back into the ocean. But no matter how many times the waves are pushed back, they keep returning. They never give up. I wish I could be more like the waves.

"There is nothing that will not be done for you while you are here. I want this to be perfect."

Uncle Kevin interrupts my thoughts.

"Now we are only here for a few days, but I want you to make every single second count. Nothing is off-limits. Nothing, I tell you. They got all kinds of stuff here. Take advantage of everything. Enjoy."

He carelessly throws countless stacks of crisp money onto the bed, tips his hat, and walks away. Dixie and I rush to the bedroom like little kids and feverishly dig through our suitcase for the forbidden swimsuits we bought at JCPenney. We leave trails of clothes on a pathway from the bathroom to the door as we rush downstairs to the beach.

We slowly sink our scantily clad bodies into beach chairs, and we cover our toes with cold, wet sand. We are served countless colorful drinks with fanciful decorations of itty-bitty umbrellas and all things maraschino cherries. I am happy.

Dixie lovingly reaches over and tenderly grabs my hand.

"Ruby Jane, I am so glad that I am here. But I am even happier that I am here with you. I love you."

"I love you too."

"Promise me one thing."

"Of course."

I am a bit wary, seeing as how the last time I agreed to something like this, it involved a dead cop on the bathroom floor of a discount coupon motel room.

"Promise me that no matter what happens, we will… I just don't know how to say it. Promise me that no matter what—"

"You know I will do anything for you. What is it?"

Her hesitation makes my blood pulse.

"Promise me that no matter what, we are about to get Mexico fucked up," Dixie screams as she slams her drink down her throat and silly-snorts.

I bellow over in laughter—not because she is hysterically funny but because I am most grateful to Andy Gibb Jesus that she doesn't make me promise to bury another Bobby Ray Montgomery.

*****

I wake up. The brilliant sun shines through the drapes in my room. In my mind, I am dead and floating in the elegance of hell. Or maybe I am alive and simply hoping for death. My head resonates with the pattern and the beating of African conga drums, and my mouth reflects the Sahara. I raise my head to the best of my ability to assess the damage and consequences of a blackout bucket of bad decisions.

I am actually not completely naked. Compared to my past blackouts? This is to be considered a significant success. I am partially clothed—clothed in cigarette ashes that have managed their way into an intriguing pattern of gray splotches all over my body.

I am most confident that the cigarette ash collection series has molded itself into the shape of the perfect elephant ear on my right thigh. Africa. It looks like Africa.

To my immediate relief, I am conveniently located in my hotel room. Score. Ruby Jane, 1. Mexico, 0.

I carefully attempt to crawl out of bed, but my excursion takes me over three smaller hills of naked bodies, all of which have yet to be identified.

"Dixie," I whisper, which is most easy considering my body won't allow more than this feat considering the dehydration ratio of tequila-to-water equation.

"Dixie," I whisper again with a bit more urgency.

I manage to pull myself over the body land mine and make my way to the bathroom. I do take time to sightsee along the way, fascinated by the visible party remnants. We must have had a great time last night, and I don't even know it.

"Ruby Jane!"

Dixie is lying on the couch with a snow-white towel over her forehead. She is naked from the waist up; and her body is surrounded with empty bottles, small bags of white powder, spoons, and syringes.

"Shhh," she whispers and then begins to laugh. "Good morning, sweet pea. You remember Umberto. Say hola, Umberto!"

She nudges the unidentified man, who is completely naked lying next to her on the couch.

Dixie sits up, reaches to the coffee table next to her, slams the drink from last night, and laughs hysterically as I try to understand any humor in my pain and suffering. The man next to her does not move or speak. I literally bend down to check his breathing. This ain't my first or second Dixie rodeo when it comes to men who may or may not be breathing.

Dixie bends her head back and out loud cackles like nothing I have ever heard.

"Do you like him, Ruby Jane? Do you like Umberto? Isn't he the sweetest?"

Dixie places her palm underneath his chin to raise him from the dead like Lazarus.

"Well, I've never met him, and I don't know him, for fuck's sake, Dixie. But I do know that..."

I am interrupted by Umberto as he rises up and slowly shakes his head and comes into consciousness. He gradually sits up and wipes his eyes like he is trying to see things as clearly as I am. I wish him good luck with that.

"Buenos dias, mi amor."

He lovingly kisses Dixie on the cheek.

"Yes, whatever. You and all of you need to go," I say. "Take your friends, amigos, or whatever. It is time to go."

"Ruby, you cannot just kick him out! That is rude. Besides, we are family. Remember, we are family first, and you know that. We don't do that to family."

"Oh, fuck. Oh no no no no no."

I grab the temple of my head with both hands and shake as last night slowly becomes clear in my head.

"Oh, fuck, Dixie. Oh, fuck. Oh, fuck. Oh, fuck. What did you do?"

"Me? I didn't do shit."

Dixie is laughing hysterically and sits up to catch her breath.

She snorts and lifts herself off the couch.

"Oh, Ruby Jane, you always seem to crack me up."

My head is swimming with the drugs and the tequila and the sex and the things that we will never talk about.

"Dixie, get rid of him," I say, determined.

"Well, Ruby, you get rid of him," she says, mocking me in the same tone.

"He's your husband. You're the one who married him."

And just like that, Mexico has become complicated.

*****

Uncle Kevin sits quietly in morning contemplation, sipping his coffee. I assume it is contemplation. He may be praying, which seems like a really good idea considering our unplanned Amnesia Matrimony Vows. I see his mind racing, and he is in deep thought. But if Uncle Kevin is angry, I cannot tell.

"How can something be bound by law if no one remembers?" I continue, pleading my case. "I don't even remember it. I was not in my right mind. I don't even remember it. Therefore, it cannot be legal! I mean, one minute we were all just partying and having fun, and then I think we were..."

I am racking my brain for the next sentence.

"I think we went—"

WEEDS THROUGH THE FLOORBOARDS

Uncle Kevin cuts me off.

"Be quiet, Ruby Jane. Let me think. I cannot think when you are talking."

He sounds impatient.

"Oh, mi senorita, es bery legal. I make sure."

Umberto basks in his newfound marriage—a marriage he understands will bring him tremendous opportunity and more money than he has ever dreamed.

"Shhh. Now, Ruby, just relax. Everything is gonna be okay," Dixie encourages.

"Well, you all know I am the last person to judge any human placed on this earth. I am a man of God. But, Ruby Jane," Uncle Kevin finally says, "for goodness' sake, married? Did you really have to marry a Mexican?"

"Ahem."

Umberto clears his throat.

"A Mexican, you say? Essa problema?"

"Oh, heavens, no. We are a loving and giving family, and we don't want there to be any confusion. We just...well...this was most unplanned, and we..." Kevin attempts to add.

"What I think Kevin is trying to say," Dixie interrupts to save the day, "is that while we are most considerate of your circumstances, Umberto, and also that we had an incredibly good evening, well, we would ask that you understand your unique position in that our sweet Ruby Jane was most inebriated, as we all were, and perhaps—"

"Oh no, no, no, no, no. You dunno," Umberto responds. "In Mexico, we married."

"In God's eyes, you are not," Uncle Kevin concludes.

"Oh, Misser Kebin, we are," Umberto continues.

"I am real sorry to hear that, Umberto. Just real sorry. I was sincerely hoping we could work this out for the sake of all of us involved. But you have made your point and I respect that."

"Why you say that?" Umberto replies.

Umberto leans his head back and laughs as if to mock Uncle Kevin.

Oh, sweet Jesus, if he only knew.

*****

Our final day is coming to an end. I sit on the sand, watching the waves crashing on the shore, meeting my human needs and then pulling them back into the ocean to settle for evaluation, then spitting them back again to me over and over and over. It seems like I'm offered a new chance each time the white-foamed film wave brushes its way against my feet.

The sun seeps deep into my pale skin. I sit with my face directly facing the sun in efforts to feel pain, to feel anything at all. The burn is comfortable for me. I am safe with pain. I like the sand. It removes layers of dead everything. It just doesn't remove memories.

Why is it that the memories we try so hard to forget are the ones that hang on to us and drown us with every thought?

Uncle Kevin is lounging in his chair while furiously making notes for his upcoming sermons and whatnots. He writes endlessly and compassionately as if each composing stroke of the pen determines our future.

Aunt Dixie sips a deadly concoction of all things Mexaholic from a real live coconut with a lime-green umbrella providing partial coverage of the liquid. Umberto calmly lies next to her and brushes her hand with his index finger as he smiles and rubs his other hand up and down her arm. I am jealous, but not because he is my Mexico-Don't-Remember Husband. I would appreciate anyone touching me so passionately and gently.

Uncle Kevin removes his hat, stands, and gathers all for his impending sermonizing.

"I love all of you, each and every one. But your Uncle Kevin needs his rest. I look forward to seeing you all in the morning. All as in you too, Umberto. You are now such an important part of our family, and God has blessed us by adding you to our most precious flock—that of a family. And you will never know how much your love means to us."

"Thank you, Misser Kebin."

Umberto smiles, as he understands the family has just welcomed him into a world of things he has never known—a world of wealth and luxury, a world of asking for nothing ever again, and a world of righteousness and repentance.

But if truth be told, anyone reading this understands at this point that life will go on. It will just go on without Uh-Oh Umberto.

And as we board the plane the next morning, I cannot help but feel some sort of sick belonging to something. I have never been accepted for me—as gay, as loving Dewayne, as loving Netti, or as loving anyone.

But today, I feel a small shell of belonging wrap the corner of my heart in a way that I have never ever felt. I do have a new title that I am most grateful for: widow. Thank you, Hey Seuss.

Chapter 6

ACHILLES' HEEL

February in Arkansas brings nothing but ice and frozen everything, and my heart is soon to be frozen in ways that it will never thaw or recover from.

It is morning. Dixie graciously sips Jack Daniel's straight from the bottle and wipes the residual with her wrist.

"Morning," she says.

Her tone sounds defeated.

"Good morning! What's going on? Dixie?"

"I need to ask you a question, Ruby Jane, and I want you to be totally honest. Can you do that for me?"

"Yes, I can. What is it?"

It has been nine weeks since we've returned from Mexico, and Dixie has been slowly declining. She won't eat. She doesn't sleep. I wake at all hours of the night to find her roaming the yard behind the trailer, talking to herself, chain-smoking cigarettes, and having conversations with people who are simply not there.

WEEDS THROUGH THE FLOORBOARDS

One evening, I woke up in the middle of the night and found her in the backyard, shadowboxing, screaming, and waving her hands like she was swatting bats. I am worried about her.

"Dixie," I say with compassion and concern.

I reach for her hand, which she warmly accepts.

"What can I do for you? Do you need me to call Uncle Kevin?"

"No, I don't need you to call Kevin. I just fucking need you to be honest!"

She raises her voice.

"Okay, okay. Everything is okay. What is it?"

"Will we ever matter? To anyone, Ruby Jane?"

"You matter to me, Dixie. You know that. You are all I have. I need you, Dixie."

"No, we don't matter. We will never matter, Ruby Jane. We are trash. Don't matter how much money we have or how many times we sit in that church pew or how much I work to do better for myself. We will always be nothin' more than trash. Why is everything so hard, Ruby Jane?"

Her voice is pathetic and cracks as she tries to hold back her desperation.

"You know what I want? I just want to...to be free. We ain't fucking free! We can't be free here in this place. No one will let us. We can only be free when we leave."

"What do you mean leave? Like, we should move away and start over? I kinda like the thought of that."

She sits up and wipes her runny nose with the sleeve of her shirt.

"Listen to me."

She softly embraces my face with her hands.

"As long as we breathe air from this earth, as long as we stay here, we will never ever be accepted. We are trash. You will always be someone that will never belong. But, Ruby, you are more than that. Think about it. All you ever wanted was to love someone. You wanted to give them your all. And look where you are. Look where that has gotten you, us.

"We are unwanted. I hate my life. I hate every day that I wake up and cannot breathe. I am so tired, Ruby Jane. I have spent my entire miserable life fighting…fighting for nothing. I am not a nobody."

Her voice trails off, and her eyes are brimming with tears. I reach over and hug her tight, because as sad as this moment is for both of us, it is the brutal honesty that only she and I understand.

Dixie looks directly into my eyes, but this time, it is different. It brings a sudden chill up and down my spine.

"But you know what? Everything is gonna be okay. I am so tired, Ruby Jane. I just need to rest. I love you, baby girl."

She kisses me as she smiles from ear to ear. She is so beautiful when she smiles.

Three hours later, I find Dixie Anne Thomas lying peacefully on her bed. She is wearing my favorite Jon Bon Jovi T-shirt and has a one-inch Pall Mall cigarette butt in her right hand. Her hair is brushed gently across her face, and she is gone.

You would think, dear reader, that I would be devastated and alarmed by the unexpected death of my sweet Dixie Anne. But truth be told, I am so proud of her. She left on her terms, and I will leave on mine.

And then there were two.

*****

Some people say that the change of seasons brings all things new. I would like to think that's true. I like the comforting thought of starting over with a new season. It's kinda like shaking the Etch A Sketch.

Summer brings to me new flowers and blooming, living things in my very own Jesus Saves Garden that I have planted right next to Dixie's trailer. I spend countless hours there, listening to the wind rustle the old, rusted tin that needs to be replaced on top of the trailer. I spend even more hours ripping up the weeds in the garden that refuse to live, and anger overwhelms me.

I miss her. I miss everything about her.

There was no funeral. Funerals are reserved for heaven-worthy believers. I scattered her ashes and buried them in the Jesus Saves Garden, along with all our secrets, each one covering the one from before like gently formed layers of shame, guilt, and regret.

I have not set foot back in the church since Dixie left us, and while the congregants offer half-assed condolences and bullshit promises, they are irresponsible and disingenuous.

"It was bound to happen sooner or later."

"Perhaps this was best."

"She is in a better place than that life she was living."

"It just takes time."

I spend my days attending not only to my garden but also to my insane, endless addictions. I am not complaining. I enjoy being numb and thoughtless. On some days, I sit on the front porch and allow all the pain to completely take over. It numbs the pain from being left here, being left behind.

*****

It is a Thursday. The brutal rapping on the front door feels feverish and urgent. Whoever is on the other side of that door makes me feel needed for the first time in a very long time. I wait. I like feeling needed.

"Ruby Jane Clancy! You have exactly one minute to open this goddamn door, or I am calling the police!" the voice informs me on the other side.

I crack the door and peer at my partner for the potential Redneck Fistfight of the Day. Old Brother Bill from the church attempts to fit his pudgy, aged body onto the tiny concrete landing that leads to the door while he leans over in attempts to see through the window.

"What the fuck do you want?" I ask through the two-inch gap.

"Open the door."

He sounds kind but angry. Is this bait and switch?

"I absolutely will not. There ain't no reason on this earth for you to be here. Now go away!"

I slam the door shut with full force.

"Now!"

Brother Bill raises his voice to an alarming level. I am not afraid because he is screaming. Why, I've heard him scream for years 'bout going to hell from the pulpit. This is way different. This scream prompts me to double-check to make sure he ain't carrying knives, duct tape, or a shovel.

I open the door and use my arm to dramatically usher him into the trailer.

"Come right on in."

Brother Bill straightens his tie as if redressing his nerve to enter such a sinful den of iniquity. I am thrilled that his entrance provides him a tour of exactly what might happen if you fuck with Andy Gibb Jesus. This will be the closest thing to happiness poor Brother Bill will ever experience.

The trailer is warmly decorated in a collage of illicit drugs and an elaborate museum of shiny liquor bottles.

"What do you want? What? You here to pray with me? To bring me back to the flock? To spread the Word? Want me to spread my legs? Huh? Answer me!"

"I need to talk to you about your uncle."

He shifts his feet from side to side. I make him nervous. Good.

"Why? What happened? Is everything okay? Is he okay?"

"Well, that is what I am trying to find out. Ruby, do you know where your uncle is?"

"Why would I know where he is?"

"When did you see him last?"

"I don't remember," I honestly answer him, as I am legitimately trying to remember the last time I spoke with him. "Why? What is going on?"

"Ruby, I need you to listen to me. Your uncle Kevin is missing. No one has seen him in over a month, not one word. I need you to tell me exactly where he is, because I know"—he immediately corrects himself—"we all know that you know. We also all know that you had something to do with this."

"Well, did you call the fucking police? How is he missing for over a month, and no one calls the police? What is wrong with you?

WEEDS THROUGH THE FLOORBOARDS

He could be dead! Did you go to Momma's house? Did you check the hospital? He could be hurt!"

I am officially in full panic mode. My heart is racing and feels like it will jump out of my chest, and my feelings are finding their way to my eyes.

Brother Bill takes a deep breath and calmly sits at the kitchen table. It is at this moment that I see that he clearly has not slept in days, and he is exhibiting a look on his face of complete distress. He stares blankly into nothingness. He randomly leans over and picks up a leftover beer from God only knows when and brings it slowly to his lips.

This act alone makes me feel utter sadness for him, because I know that he has never had a sip of beer or a good blow job from any male or female. He swallows the expired suds and exhales loudly.

"Ruby, all of the money is gone."

"W-wh-what do you mean? All the money? All of what money?"

"THE money, Ruby. The only money. Don't even act like you don't understand."

His face is now red, and the veins in his neck are popping out.

"The entire church fund. It is gone. The cash…investments… all of it is gone. The insurance money from the rebuild, the cash from the safe, it is all gone. Now I am only gonna ask you one more time. Where is he?"

"I don't know where he is, and I have no idea what you are talking about. Look around you."

I raise my arms and present him to my inherited trailer of despair and poverty.

"You think I had anything to do with this? You think that I am living the high life on your fucking money? You piece of shit! Get the fuck out of my house!"

Brother Bill calmly stands and confidently walks toward the door.

"Ruby, if you hear from him, you need to call me. You hear me?"

"And why the fuck would I do that?"

"Because he is in a lot of trouble, Ruby, and you don't want to be a part of that."

"Oh, really? So what? No one fucking cares about your money. So what if he left? What am I supposed to do about it? I certainly don't care! Y'all never cared about me. How dare you come to my house and ask me for fucking help! You have some nerve! Now get out of my house."

Brother Bill turns to me in his last recruitment effort.

"Just so you know, Ruby, he took everything."

"Whatever. That is what he does! He preaches and recruits and manipulates and then takes all your devil pocket money and hides it. That's what he's been doing his entire life. He is a professional. And let me tell you this. You will never find him. And I am doing you a favor by telling you this. He is dangerous. You don't want to find him. Trust me. Uncle Kevin cannot be found unless he wants to be found."

"Nine hundred thousand dollars is simply not a whatever, Ruby Jane."

He senses the shock on my face.

"Find him," he says firmly. "And when you do? God will reward you greatly. And if you don't find him, God will not reward you at all. He will take something from you, something you care about and love. You understand what I am saying to you, Ruby?"

"Are you threatening me? Is that what this is? 'Cause I ain't afraid of you."

I slowly walk to him and press my body as close as I can without touching him. I reach down and place my lips to his sweaty neck and put my left hand on his crotch and rub slowly up and down. Brother Bill remains motionless, and I can hear his breathing as he tries to steady his body and, more than likely, his mind.

"You can't take nothin' from someone who's got nothin'," I breathlessly whisper against his neck. "But if you ever come here again?" I continue as I rub harder. "I will cut your dick off and mount it as a Jesus trophy on my wall."

WEEDS THROUGH THE FLOORBOARDS

Brother Bill violently slaps my hand away. He is sweating, and his face is flushed. He turns rapidly to open the door and stares me right in the eyes.

"You heard what I said. Find him. And when you do? There will be a reward."

He leaves me standing alone in the living room, speechless. I realize that my legs are shaking uncontrollably, and the air has left the room.

I begin wildly imagining my feared consequences of this imminent threat. Would they lock me up? Put me in the Yell County Jail? Shoot me? Hang me? I sincerely hope for the latter. I like the thought of the pain it will bring.

But even this illogical, vivid fantasy playing out in my head cannot erase the uncompromising truth that my uncontrollable Uncle Kevin is on the run, and Big Boy Brother Bill can still get his dick up, WAY up, if in the future the need ever arises.

*****

The next evening I spend in a security blanket of warmth and need and lust and desire and grief, hand-delivered to me by licking my open wounds, sucking my nipples, rubbing my clit, embracing my entire body, and holding tight to the only thing I have left.

Netti has obviously been lesbian training on the side, because when she comes nightly and enters my bed, I cannot turn her down for any reason. She shows up at all hours of the night—with a man, a woman, another man, a black man, two women, two men, strangers I have never met, and people I have known for years.

Our bodies all spill together and dissolve into an endless lake of all things wet and yearning and needed, and it fills me with what I am lacking. We dissolve drugs into our desires and make every attempt to not care if we wake up as long as we have one another.

I spend my days feverishly deciding how I will ever find Uncle Kevin or if he will contact me. The possible scenarios play over and over and over in my head. I cannot sleep. I am being followed at all times and watched if I do something as small as water the garden.

I suppose my heart is broken, because I cry a lot. I am a fucking fool. I never dreamed that Uncle Kevin would leave me. Never.

What they don't tell you about life is that when you are not normal, it is judgmental, arrogant, and hate-filled. In this life, you are not allowed to be who you are. You will never be good enough. You will never fit into the mold that man has made. You will never amount to anything. You will never be able to love.

I often wonder, why would God, in all his majesty, bring me into this existence only to suffer? Why would he create me in his image and likeness and make me the way that I am? I can't help how I am. Trust me, I've tried to be different.

And what they don't tell you about death is that when this world makes you fight and keeps you constantly disappointed for doing the only thing you could ever know, then death can be a beautiful thing. Death releases you from a world that hates you and does not understand who God made you to be.

It is a Tuesday. I have always hated Tuesdays. Tuesdays are careless.

I spend my morning weeding my Jesus Saves Garden and pretend-talking to Aunt Dixie. I am on my knees, pulling the last of the long bright-green onion grass. When I glimpse to the right side of the garden, there is a deliberate patch of weeds invading and attempting to take over my finally beautiful Jesus Saves Garden. Grandma would be proud.

Weeds are peculiar. They are a force to be reckoned with. They are deeply rooted and do not give up, just like waves. But it's okay, because like these weeds, I am strong. And even though they are pulled and ripped apart by their roots, they continuously come back, just like me.

I shift my body to the right in an effort to remove this particular group, which brings my mind to a pause. The green grass surrounding their roots is a different color, and as I look closer, I can see that the ground has been broken and is uneven.

I grab my shovel and remove the top layer of soil. Then I clearly see it. The sun bounces a brilliant light off the top of a shiny-silver lid, which is attached to a Mason jar. I delicately bring the jar from the ground and unscrew the lid.

There, folded neatly and placed at the bottom, is a white envelope. My hands shake as I lift it out of the jar and slowly open it. Money falls like raindrops to the ground. I grab feverishly at all the bills and shove them back into the envelope while looking all around to make sure I am unnoticed. I am good at being unnoticed.

My hands shake violently as I open the white paper that fell out with the money.

Dearest Ruby Jane,

I knew you would come, but I must go. Bury every memory here where it is safe, and then you will be free.

Uncle Kevin

While you would think I would be relieved to know that my Uncle Kevin is still alive, I am actually hurt that he left me. Everyone always leaves, and once again, I am all alone.

It's okay. I am used to it. It is better for me to be alone than be surrounded by people who don't understand me.

And then there was one.

Chapter 7

MR. POE

The brick building resembling burnt toast is isolated and remote, nestled intentionally off the main road, so efforts to remain invisible are possible. I am used to being invisible.

The perfect square gold welcome sign is mounted on the side of the glass entry door and reads, "Dr. Raven Miller, MD, LPC." The feminine font is exquisite and formal, like a private invitation to a much celebratory ball.

And while I would like to think that Dr. Miller is well-known to me due to her astounding résumé and endless doctoral credentials, I literally chose the name from the faded yellow pages of the Yell County phone book because deep down inside, I like the thought of a human being named Raven.

> ra-ven
> noun:
> a large heavily built crow with mainly black
> plumage

WEEDS THROUGH THE FLOORBOARDS

The waiting area is secretive and soundless. There is no receptionist. There are no other patients. There is nothing to offer me protection other than myself. I am having a real-life *Lord of the Flies* moment.

There are, however, three worn, weary, tattered leather chairs and a coffee table that attempts to hold the latest issues of *Just Seventeen* and *Tiger Beat*.

The door opens.

"Ruby?"

Dr. Miller gently peeks out and looks to me and smiles. She is not black, as her name implies.

Strike One.

"Yes, ma'am."

"Please," she says calmly, "come with me."

She leads me into a back office that has an exquisite shelf inundated with books and pictures. I pause to resonate on them and then assume they are her family. They are all smiling and look so happy. I cautiously wonder if perhaps these are the individuals they sell in the frame to influence a buyer to purchase it. It is simply far too perfect.

I apprehensively stand, attempt to collect my nerves, and follow Dr. Miller to the chamber of All Things Right. Truth be told? I ain't scared of nothing. But right at this exact moment? I am scared. And although I wish to reconsider my personal decisions to seek out professional directions, Dr. Miller wastes no time.

Dr. Miller sits astutely behind her oak desk and motions for me to take the chair directly in front of her. She picks up a pen and jots what appears to be items of utmost importance onto a school bus yellow legal pad.

"So, Ruby, can you share with me what brings you here today?" she asks.

"I...well...I wanted to kind of talk to someone. Well, you, of course, a professional, because I am not okay, and I just don't even know where to begin...or what it is that you can do for me."

"Perfect. You are doing a great job, Ruby. Can you share with me how long you have felt this way?"

I crush my hands under my bottom to prevent them from shaking violently. I shift from the right side of the chair to the left, and then I continue.

"My whole life. There's just not a time I can remember feeling like I belong here, and that is why I am here. I am, well, I am completely alone, and I was hoping that someone could help me feel better or maybe help me to understand."

"Well, Ruby, I am so glad you came. You are in the right place. What I can do is work with you, and we can talk through some specific strategies that will help you cope and feel better about your life and all of your situations. Does that interest you?"

"Yes, ma'am," I answer, relieved.

"I do, however, charge for my services, and—"

I cut her off immediately.

"That won't be a problem, ma'am. I can pay you."

"Well, then, sounds like we have a dependable, solid plan. It is very important for you to understand that there is nothing wrong with reaching out to others for help. We all need help, and the stigma associated with asking can be overwhelming. So I would like to start with just a few questions. Do you smoke or drink?"

"No, ma'am."

I literally shift to ensure lightning will not strike my sinful soul dead on the spot and set this whole motherfucker up in flames.

"What about drugs, Ruby? Any illegal drugs?"

"Absolutely not, ma'am."

Again, I anxiously wait for someone, anyone, like Cagney and Lacey, to bust down the door with a list of every drug I've ever ingested and put me on a performance stage and call me a Liar, Liar, Pants On Fire.

"Okay, good. Thank you for telling me the truth. That's important, because if need be, I can sometimes provide patients with medication to help with their feelings."

"Really?" I inquire.

I am officially interested. Drugs? Hell yeah. She is speaking my addiction language.

"So let's get started. First, anything and everything you say to me during our sessions will be held in total confidence. Nothing we talk about will ever leave these four walls. So always feel free to speak your mind. If I am going to help you, Ruby, you have to be brutally honest."

"Yes, ma'am. I can do that."

I can be honest, except when it comes to Refrigerator Bobby or Oil Boy or ol' Roy or Brother Eddie or Senor Umberto.

Strike Two.

"Can you perhaps provide me a little bit of background to start with? Maybe we can start with some of your most recent feelings, and then we can go from there."

"Well, I feel like I am not accepted and don't belong here, mostly because I don't, well, I feel different."

"Can you explain what you mean by different?"

"I mean, like, in the girl way. I feel different."

"Would you care to elaborate? I am not sure that I fully understand."

"Oh, okay. Well, I like girls in that way. I actually am in love with one, and I want to marry her one day. I have always been this way since as long as I can remember, and because of it, no one ever accepted me, not my momma or my daddy. Well, maybe Dixie Anne, but she's dead now."

"So just to clarify, Ruby, what I am hearing from you is that you are feeling unaccepted by your family and society because you like girls in a sexual way?"

"Yes, that is exactly what I am saying."

I feel relieved that Dr. Raven Miller hears me. I mean, really hears me.

Dr. Miller brings her pen up from the paper she is writing on and calmly places the paper and pen down on her desk. I anxiously await her words of wisdom and understanding and her acceptance. But more importantly, I am confident that for the first time in my life, I have made a decision in my favor.

And then Dr. Raven Miller looks softly at me and says, "Well, Ruby, can you blame them? You are for sure going to hell."

Strike Three.

And that was my first and last day of trying to get right.

Chapter 8

A RIVER RUNS THROUGH ME

There is a moment in our lives when we face the full realization that any and all things will be made right, and this particular Friday will forever be written in history as the most beautiful day of my life.

I wake up early—so early that the morning birds have yet to sing and the morning sun has yet to shine. It is a beautiful day.

I carelessly arrange myself on the front porch of the trailer with a fifth of Jim Beam and a half of whatever cocaine leftovers can be found strewn around the trailer. Today is different from any other day, because today, I have made a decision—a decision to finally make a change. I realize that I have been waiting all this time for others to change. Today, I will be the one to change.

I sit quietly and listen to the sounds of the world waking up around me. It's amazing what we can really hear when we decide to really listen. I walk to the back to tend to my Jesus Saves Garden for what I know will be my last time, embracing the full fragrance of jasmine, honeysuckle, mint, and roses.

WEEDS THROUGH THE FLOORBOARDS

Weeds have overtaken most of the garden, much like how the weeds have overtaken my soul and my heart. I try to remember that at one time, weeds were flowers—flowers that never allowed anyone to know them and finally gave up because they were unloved and not accepted. They wouldn't and couldn't flourish.

I am so much like them. I am unloved and not accepted, and I, too, could not become what I wanted to be.

I find a piece of white paper and neatly write with my best penmanship my letter to the world. I leave it folded on the front porch, underneath the bright ruby that was once given to me by Aunt Dixie.

I cannot remember a time when I have ever been happier. I spend my entire day in an unfamiliar feeling of relief. I dress in my favorite pair of shorts and my purple shirt from the lost and found. I still have it. It brings me comfort.

And as the evening sun sets brilliantly over the horizon, I don't pity myself that I am still alive at the end of the day, because change is coming.

I realize that I actually cherish the feeling of this sunset. The sun has a determination to completely end something that others feel might be worthy of staying. It takes time for a sun to completely disappear and set in the sky, just like how it takes time for people to change.

I grab the keys to Dixie's station wagon and head to the river behind the Pine Creek Pentecostal Church, the windows down, the wind blowing my hair. And when I am certain that no one is around to ruin my perfect day, I calmly wade into the cool water of the river, where I hear the droplets bubble across the rocks and pebbles that cover the beds.

I submerge my entire body into the cleansing water, a smile on my face. I wade deeper so that the weights can do their job. And then I breathe in and out, in and out. The water fills my lungs and expands into the holes that so many people have dug into my life. It is not at all painful or terrible. It is beautiful.

I breathe in and out effortlessly. And then I see it, the infinite world below me, revealed with an inexplicable brilliance. Peace and warmth and love fill me with every breath I take, each breath bringing me closer to what most reading this story would consider my end. But rest assured, there is no end here. This is really my beginning. I am free.

Dear world,

My name is Ruby Jane Clancy. You will find me in the river, if you care to look. I only ask that you bury me next to my momma and daddy... facin' west.

ABOUT THE AUTHOR

Jonna Trusty-Patterson grew up in rural Arkansas and graduated from Baylor University in Waco, Texas, with a degree in business administration. Before entering into the field of education, she became a professional photographer and still spends time at her studio.

She has lived in Houston for the past twenty-six years. She currently teaches English language arts at an inner-city all-girls school in Houston's Third Ward. She has two sons, John Thomas and Jackson. Her wife, Kimmy, is a high school counselor and was her inspiration to write her very first novel.

Printed in the USA
CPSIA information can be obtained
at www.ICGtesting.com
LVHW050831290524
781182LV00002B/249

9 781637 843659